THE STARS CAN WAIT

THE
STARS
CAN
WAIT

a novel

✦

Jay Basu

Henry Holt and Company   New York

Henry Holt and Company, LLC
Publishers since 1866
115 West 18th Street
New York, New York 10011

Henry Holt ® is a registered trademark of
Henry Holt and Company, LLC.

Library of Congress Cataloging-in-Publication Data
Basu, Jay.
The stars can wait : a novel / Jay Basu.—1st ed.
    p.   cm
ISBN 0-8050-6887-2(hb)
    1. Silesia, Upper (Poland and Czech Republic)—Fiction.
2. World War, 1939–1945—Silesia, Upper (Poland and Czech
Republic)—Fiction.   3. Teenage boys—Fiction.   4. Brothers—
Fiction.   I. Title.

PS3602.A85 S74 2002
813'.6—dc21   2001024843

Henry Holt books are available for special
promotions and premiums. For details contact:
Director, Special Markets.

First Edition 2002

Designed by Paula Russell Szafranski

Printed in the United States of America

1   3   5   7   9   10   8   6   4   2

To Ann, Dipak, and Laura Basu,

to my darling T. K.,

to Becky Strzeja,

and to Paul Strzeja, without whose story

this one could never have been written

The incense was to heaven dear,

Not as a perfume, but a tear.

And stars show lovely in the night,

But as they seem the tears of light.

—*Andrew Marvell, "Eyes and Tears"*

The village of Maleńkowice does not exist and has never existed; its surroundings and its likenesses, however, are real. The region of Eastern Europe known as Silesia, settled in the Middle Ages by Germans and Poles, belonged variously to the Kingdom of Poland, Bohemia, the Austrian Habsburgs, and Prussia. In 1918, as Polish independence came into existence, the Polish-speaking populace of Upper Silesia, east of the Oder River, expressed their desire to become part of Poland proper. After three Polish uprisings and a plebiscite, the region was divided chiefly between Poland and Germany, with Poland acquiring barely one-seventh of the original landmass of all Silesia. On this small slip of earth, our story unfolds.

THE
STARS
CAN
WAIT

One

On an autumn night in 1940, one year into German occupation, in a Polish mining village called Maleńkowice within the area known as Upper Silesia, a fifteen-year-old boy named Gracian Sófka sat poised and upright on his bed watching his sleeping brother. He breathed carefully and with respect for the silence, each breath composing itself into a white cloud, blooming and then fading into the cold air. His brother, Paweł, twelve years his elder, whispered in his sleep, a single long strip of moonlight tracing over his cheek and pillow. When Gracian was sure that sleep was absolute, he swung his legs slowly round and let his feet rest upon the floorboards. He reached down, hands fumbling in the dark, and pulled on his woollen trousers and a heavy sweater over his nightshirt and then his shoes, pausing now and again to let the low creaks of the mattress resolve themselves into silence. Then he stood and walked to the door, unhung his coat, and hunched it on. He patted the pocket to feel the bulk of its special cargo, waited with one hand on the rim of the open door for nothing, for the right time perhaps, and then slipped out.

In the hall he walked too noisily past the room in which his mother slept. At the end of the hall was a window. The moonlight painted pale oblongs onto the dirty wood. Downstairs slept his older sister and her husband and their baby and some of the animals who were locked into the kitchen out of the cold. He reached the window. He undid the catch and eased the lower frame up as far as he needed. The wood was old, and tiny white flakes tumbled down onto his hands. A gap had opened in the night and his heart was already beating through it.

He climbed out with an ease that was practiced, turned himself around on the ledge and knelt and gripped the wood, then he lowered himself slowly down until he was hanging by his fingers flat against the wall of the house. The night was black and faultless and a chill breeze pricked at his skin. He reached out with one hand toward the crab-apple tree that grew in the yard and felt the rough cold bark of the nearest limb and held it tight. He gave a slight kick against the wall and then swung his other arm through space and clamped that hand around the branch and he was free, the whole canopy shifting with his weight and the red leaves rustling, cascading, a crimson snow melting into the shadows below. He edged down the branch until he reached the trunk and let himself fall and thud onto solid ground.

Then he ran. He ran through the darkened yard, vaulting the wall there, and across the rise of field beyond, his shadow arcing up to catch him in the moonlight, his breath alive and white, up toward the forest edge. There were no patrols in the field, but once he reached the forest he needed to be careful.

The darkness of the forest was like no other, and the silence was not that of death but of the watching of things. The boy knew his way and moved as if following a path or thread of shadow visible only to himself. He weaved through trees and thickets, listening to the scuffling of his feet and the rasp of his breathing, tripping through blackness toward his goal. From somewhere further within the many kilometres of forest, further than he had dared to venture, came a brief ticklish rumble, and he knew that German vehicles were out there moving around the small outbuildings of the army base.

Less than halfway there, he heard the sound of voices and of feet less careful than his own. And after that came a sudden sweep of flashlight against the trees, becoming two distinct haloes quivering and breaking and rebreaking, and the voices coming nearer speaking German to each other in hushed bursts. Gracian moved himself behind a thick pine and let the night consume him. The two men came nearer, their flashlights probing. In the dark the boy's chest heaved and his throat burned and the muscles in his legs were wire-tight. The men were very close, their footsteps seeming to sound inside his head, and the lights were leaping and idling around the closest trees and picking out the furrowed bark, and then they reached the place where the boy waited. He closed his eyes. He could hear the men pausing, muttering about the cold, and could feel the light curling, extending around the heavy trunk, trying to reach his face and tear it from the darkness.

The light was gone and the men were leaving. The boy waited and craned his head around the trunk. Two men. Olive coats and black pistol holsters. The patrol.

Again he was running. Deep into the forest to the viewing place, the place he had been coming to since he was twelve years old. A tiny clearing only a few metres square, where the trees rose on all sides to frame the sky in an unbroken circle, as if to offer it to the earth below. When the boy reached it he threw himself down upon his back among the thick bracken and spike grass and regained his breath and let the air cool his sweat. Then he took his first real look at the sky. No clouds. A pure and boundless nothing, pinned through with one hundred billion stars. The universe gathered between treetops.

He lay there and gazed up for a long while. Then he reached into his coat pocket and pulled out the bronze-gilt magnifying glass his father had used for reading in the last months of the disease and weighed it in his hand. He reached back in and removed the small book and read again its title, eyes straining in the dim reflected starlight: WSTĘP DO ASTRONOMII, faded red letters on cream. He turned to his favourite pages, ignoring the words, and inspected the pictures there. Constellations, eighty-eight of them, their names below—names wild and restless in a language that was not his own—the River, the Furnace, the Hunting Dogs; *Eridanus, Fornax, Canes Venatici.* The Lion, the Wolf, the Southern Cross; *Leo, Lupus, Crux.*

Propping the book next to his head, he lay back down and raised the magnifier before his eyes until the ring of sky had slid behind the lens, bulging out toward him. He watched the stars swell and settle as the glass swept over them, and he looked there for the printed shapes upon the page.

In the east, the Great Bear. In the west, the Crab. He traced their shapes with his eyes, like reading.

After a while, he put down the glass and huddled in his coat for warmth and watched the sky unaided. He would have to leave soon, he knew, but the dreaminess had him and he imagined himself rising up into the expanse until he was nothing but another pinprick dancing above the world. Then a meteor shower on the northern rim of the trees sent out five or six trails reaching out and dying back, as if a golden hand had risen through the distance and tried to grasp hold of the night, and Gracian was lost completely to the wonder.

✦

By the time he heard the footfalls it was too late. He felt
two hands grip him roughly by his coat collar and he
tried to gasp, but one of the hands had clamped his mouth
shut. A man's face was upside down over his, blocking
the sky.

"You idiot."

Paweł. It was his brother, Paweł, hauling him up with
his good hand to face him. His bad hand was around Gracian's neck.

"What do you think you're doing out here after curfew?" he was saying in a low voice, his expression violent.
"Lying on the ground like a madman! Don't you know
they'll kill you if they find you? The forest is crawling
with patrols tonight, you stupid boy. *Ty idioto!*"

Paweł snatched the magnifier from his brother's hand.

When Gracian could speak he said, "But what are you—? You were *sleeping*—"

"You are a madman, do you know that?" Paweł said, dragging his brother up until they were both squatting. "Now be quiet and follow me. And *stay close*."

Paweł led his brother back through the forest a way he had never travelled before, until they were back at the house and the sun was lapping at the distant forest edge and the blackness was becoming candlelight orange. Tomorrow Gracian had to work an afternoon shift at colliery Richter, known formerly as colliery Siemianowice.

Before they climbed back through the window, Gracian turned to his brother. "Please don't tell Mother," he whispered.

Paweł placed his hands on his brother's shoulders. "I won't. This time. And you should be grateful for it until the day you die," he said.

Then he shook his head and looked hard at Gracian. "But this madness has to stop, understand?" he said. "This is the last time; I'll make sure of it. This hobby of yours is not worth your life or Mother's happiness. The stars can wait, boy—that's all they ever do."

Gracian remained silent. Then he said, "How did you find me, Paweł?"

His brother did not smile. He simply made a trough with his hands for Gracian to stand upon and told him to hurry before the sun was full.

An hour later the cockerels began to sing. It was the autumn of 1940. In a small mining village in Upper Silesia.

For the past year Gracian Sófka, fifteen years old, had been risking his skin to look at the sky.

By the time half a year had passed, Gracian would journey twice more into the deep heart of the forest, the German army would reach the French Atlantic coast, the constellations would have followed their secret paths across the universe, and Paweł Sófka would no longer be alive.

＊

Gracian was woken by his mother a little time later. She was shaking him, and when he opened his eyes he saw that bright sunlight had broken into the room. His mother tugged at his blanket.

"Get up," she was saying sternly. "You sleep too much."

Gracian saw that his brother was gone, his bed empty and neatly made, and he was suddenly afraid.

"Where's Paweł?" he said.

"Out," his mother said. "Looking for work. Now get dressed; you need to feed the animals before you go."

Paweł had not told her.

Gracian put his clothes on and went downstairs with his mother. At the table his sister, Francesca, was washing clothes in a tin bowl, the child on her knee. Her husband, Józef Kukła, had left for work. He was a baker.

Before Gracian went into the yard he checked the drawer beneath the sink and saw his father's old magnifying glass there, tucked back inside its brown cloth bag.

That Paweł had found him in the viewing place did not seem very strange to Gracian Sófka. For Paweł was a mystery—to Gracian, to his mother and sister, to the whole village. A mystery.

When Gracian was five years of age, Paweł disappeared from the family home for nine months. His mother and his father, who was still alive then, said that he had gone to live in Germany for a time. No one spoke of it, least of all his father, who would become silent at the mention of Paweł's name and remove and fold up his glasses in his big hand and stare out the window toward the shadowed forest.

Paweł returned with plans to join the Polish army. He became a corporal. He could ride horses. He left after seven years of service and came back home and secured a little leatherwork. In 1938 he volunteered again and was stationed as a mounted radio operator in southern Slovakia to help defend against the coming German invasion. His job was to ride between unit encampments with a giant coil of radio wire slung over his shoulder and lay the wire down as he rode.

There he had fought long and hard and had seen many men injured or killed. Then two days before the Germans overwhelmed the Poles, Paweł had been caught in a mortar storm. His horse was killed beneath him and two fingers from his left hand were blown off. For a while he had searched for them among the field grasses before his division found him and took him to safety. When Gracian could coax his brother to speak of his experiences in the army—rarely, for Paweł spoke little at the best of times—he would say, "What do I need two useless fingers for, boy? Now at least they're doing some good, feeding the crimson flowers by the river Hron."

When the Polish army was finally defeated, Paweł had stripped off his uniform and dressed himself up as a civilian. Where he had obtained the clothes he would never tell, though Paweł was an enterprising man, and Gracian imagined that he had persuaded one of the Slovak villagers to come to his aid.

His hand bleeding through the tight-wound bandages, turning them slowly red as the flowers of which he would speak, Paweł had started to walk. He walked, alone, up through Stredoslovensky province, following the Hron as far as Brezno, then across open land until reaching the dark Carpathians, where he sheltered among the mountain crags. Then onward toward the High Tatra peaks sheathed in dust and snow, along the lonely passes, traversing the border into Poland, where in Rabka he was able to steal a horse and ride down through rough country south of Kraców into Silesia, the horse half dead from starvation by the time the lights of Katowice could be seen. And then on foot to Maleńkowice and finally home, collapsed at the door, his bones jutting like shipwrecks beneath red-baked skin.

He had been moving for three weeks, avoiding capture. He had travelled nearly two hundred kilometres.

After his return, many men in the village asked Paweł why he had not, as others had, fled into Italy or Switzerland and rejoined the Polish forces. But Paweł never answered them, for the answer was clear. The answer he had given upon the day of his return, whispering it through lips parched and dusty at the kitchen table as his family fetched him food and water. The answer, captured pure and simple within the breadth of a single word: *"Anna . . ."*

Anna Malewska. Daughter of William and Urszula Malewska. Paweł's love and his fiancée. She was a beauty such as the village of Maleńkowice had never before witnessed. Her skin was as pale as morning milk, her parted hair two folds of black silk across her shoulders. Eyes the fragrant brown of sandalwood. A man would gladly walk the length of the world for Anna Malewska, thought Gracian, as his brother gasped her name one day a year ago, and he had closed his eyes to picture her face and felt once more that silver pang of something he could not name.

Paweł had recovered and now spent much of his time away from the house, with Anna or looking for work, although where he went and who he saw about this remained obscure. His three-fingered hand kept him from re-entering the craft professions, and he always claimed the mines were not for him. This made their mother, who was paying what she could for Paweł's upkeep, bitterly angry.

"They'll give you a job there, Paweł—I can't fend for you forever. There isn't enough," she would say.

Paweł would tut and rake his hair and fold his arms. "Just give me time, Mother. I'll find something. I never asked for your money."

"Listen." Her face calm but her voice becoming steely. "I've had about enough of your ingratitude. If the mines were good enough for your father and if they're good enough for your brother—"

And Paweł would fling back his chair, sending it tumbling across the floor, and stand up. "Well, maybe it shouldn't be good enough for Gracian! All he's doing is feeding the Germans."

His mother would be frozen then, her face red and her wooden cooking spoon drawn up into the air between them. She would not let them talk of the Germans. She was as afraid as the rest of the village.

"Don't start, Paweł," she would say in an urgent voice, her eyes wide and alarmed. "Your talk could kill us all."

He would leave. And then the silence of the house and of his mother would silt down upon Gracian, weighting his shoulders. Later, Paweł would return and apologize and embrace his mother and promise to visit the mines tomorrow, but no one believed he would.

Such was the way of Paweł Sófka. Always leaving. Never staying. There were times when Gracian was tired from work and he would sit with his brother unspeaking, feeling a great swell of desire to question him about the way in which he led his life, but something about his brother's quiet face made the words falter and drown before they left his mouth, and he would be unable to say a word and then it was too late and Paweł was up and dusting his trouser fronts with his palms and vanishing outside again—back out into the close-guarded mystery of himself.

When he was a child of six or seven Gracian had once gone through the pockets of Paweł's midnight-blue suit, which hung on its own heavy wooden hanger in the wardrobe. He was looking for a few stray złotys to buy some boiled *cukierki* with in the village. He had to stand on a chair to reach the suit, which was worn to a shine at knees and elbows as if to retain there the force of Paweł's joints, and he dipped his hands first into the trouser pockets and then under the flap of the jacket and finally up into the inside pocket. He found nothing but fluff. He tried the side pockets of the jacket, left and then right. In the right he came across something on which he stubbed his fingers. He wrapped his fingers back over it and felt the weight, the smoothness. He brought it out and spread his palm to reveal it.

The gun was small and square and only a little bigger than his hand span. The surface was silver and polished to a liquid shine, and there were a few embossed letters and numbers that he could not read. The handle was white, hard. He held it in both hands and pointed it away from him at the floor, the chair shifting and protesting on the uneven boards. He put both index fingers of both hands around the trigger and pulled hard. Something moved at the back of the weapon and there was a loud solid click that echoed. In surprise he dropped the gun, and it fell with a crack against the wood. Immediately he jumped off the chair and picked it up and pushed it back into the pocket, his heart racing, suddenly afraid of the strip of light under the door.

Gracian walked to the mines, a heaviness inside him. Paweł had said he would not let him back out into the nighttime forest, and Gracian believed this was true. A joy he had taken for himself since he was twelve years old was to be snatched away; he felt as if something too large to see whole had come to an end, before he was ready.

He walked through the village with his coat collar drawn up around his ears. Winter was coming. The day was clearer than usual, the coal-soaked air swept fresh by winds blowing cold from the north. As he passed, a German special policeman watched with eyes as pale as waterlilies.

He hung his coat in the locker room, then stripped and shrugged into his coveralls and joined the other workers in the gated forecourt. He looked at the moss and weeds growing in the cracks of the concrete as the lift came up to the surface. He stepped in with the others, and the lift plunged and his stomach floated inside him. At level four, one kilometre beneath the earth, he stepped out.

The mine was its own kind of night. But there were no stars there. There were only the wide black walls glistening and the white haloes of acetylene lamps.

The foreman had a lit cigarette stub in the corner of his mouth. Gracian listened for his designation, watching the deep orange ring of it rise and fall as the foreman spoke, and then he boarded the roofless train and swayed with its momentum until he reached his section of coal face. Gerard Dylong, his partner, was already there.

"Hello, Galileo," Dylong said.

Dylong had heard Gracian talk of the stars a thousand times. He was the only one who would listen. He slung his arm over Gracian's shoulder.

"Today we're going to blast this entire face into dust," he said.

Dylong, with his dark, creased, animal-hide skin and his bear's shoulders. Dylong, whose mind many of the men believed had been poisoned by tragedy. "Don't listen to Gerard Dylong! He's a madman! His head is sick!"

So said the men.

Dylong was fifty-three years old, the oldest miner in the whole of southern Poland. When he turned forty, close to the usual retirement age for miners, his wife had died in childbirth, and his only son with her. Dylong refused to leave work, then, and had remained at the colliery ever since.

"What am I to do at home?" he had said. "Die as well, that's what."

But no one could deny his skills as a miner, for they

were incomparable. Dylong's understanding of the coal seams appeared to verge up on telepathy. Every shift he would stand in front of the face, one thick hand upon his hip, the other cradling his chin, deep in thought. He would step forward, run his palm over the rock, click his tongue and chew his lip, and glance over at Gracian, who observed, expectant. Then he would instruct the boy exactly where to place the explosives and how much, watching in silence as the coal cascaded down in the blast, and after the dust cloud was ventilated there lay revealed a quantity of prime coal for loading. Together, Dylong and the boy could clear twice as much in a few hours as other teams could in a day.

Dylong had a theory. He believed that somewhere deep within the black tonnes of coal there lay a rich untapped reservoir of sulphur. He said he could feel its presence in his skin. He said he could feel the green mineral down deep in the bone, where the marrow was. He said that one day he would find those sulphur deposits, and they would make him the richest man in the country.

Every shift he vowed to discover sulphur, and every shift his vow was left unfulfilled.

They worked hard and with few words. Dylong completed his deliberations and then bored holes into various points of the face. Gracian prepared the explosives, lifting out the grey sticks wrapped in oilpaper, pressing the detonators into the tips, pushing them down to the lip of the bore channels. Then both men packed in the clay, soft in the dry flint, and stood back, and the blast thundered, and Dylong powered the ventilator to survey the yield. Now they could begin to brace the ceiling with damp wood slats before loading the carts.

But Gracian's mind was not on the work today. He could think only of being found out last night and of the viewing place remaining empty, tonight and every next night to come. The thought made his muscles sag and he began to drop behind in his loading, the shovel like a dead weight in his hands. Dylong noticed this and paused in his work.

"What's the matter, Galileo. Those scrawny muscles of yours finally given up?"

"Nothing," the boy said.

Dylong propped his shovel on the cart edge and folded his arms and flexed his biceps and grinned. "Cloudy last night, was it?" he said.

"Just shut up, Dylong," Gracian said.

Dylong flung out an arm and slapped the boy hard on the back of his scalp. Then he was leaning into him.

"The last man to say that to me soon regretted it," he said.

But before Gracian could speak Dylong was grinning again and winking.

"Get your head out of the sky, boy, and back where it belongs." And Dylong turned away.

After the shift was over they sat tired and dirty against the wooden props, and Dylong pulled out a pack of cigarettes, snared one in his mouth, and then passed another to Gracian, and the boy knew all was good between them because cigarettes were rationed, now, and rare. As they smoked, Gracian watched the older man, saw how he sat with his face set in sadness, and knew he was thinking again of the sulphur. Then Dylong said what he said at the end of every shift.

"Maybe next time, Galileo. There's still hope."

＋

When he got home, Paweł was not there, but the upstairs window had been sealed shut with a row of silver wood tacks. Gracian ran his hands over their sharp heads and gazed at the sky beyond the glass.

"Paweł did it," Francesca said as she came up the stairs. Her voice surprised him. "He said we needed to stop the winter draughts from coming in."

Gracian ate with his sister and mother. The women were talking about Antoni Dukaj, the son of a leather-worker in the village. Antoni Dukaj was only a little older than Gracian.

"They took him off the street, just like that," Gracian's mother was saying. "Kicking and screaming. He tried to say he was working for his father, but they wouldn't hear it. They just put him on the next train to Austria. Said he was needed to work the fields."

Francesca shook her head. "Who knows what to believe?" she said, crossing herself.

"And do you know who they say reported him?" their mother said. "Karl Holzman! That bastard's been here as long as we have, and now they come and suddenly he's a German again."

She unclasped her long grey hair and then reclasped it. Her face was grim.

"They don't even bother to lie anymore. Before they used to tell us favouring the Germans was about protection. Now they say it's about *right*. Everything's changed," she said into her plate.

Later, Gracian went to his room and looked out the small window at the stars, blinking in the haze of late evening. He reached beneath his bed, found his book on astronomy, and inspected its cover, faded red letters on cream, in the lamplight.

His brother had given him the book when he was barely eleven years old. It was a time when Paweł was on leave from the army. He had walked into their room at night, still in uniform, his figure looming inside the doorway, and tossed it onto the bed. "A present," he had said. "Perhaps you'll have a hobby now." Gracian had read it all that night, understanding what he could. Though he was a better reader than many of the other children in the village, many of the words were difficult and strange. But to his surprise he had found in the densely typed facts and diagrams a kind of opening. A chance for escape.

Now he opened the pages as he had done so many times before and saw—the River, the Furnace, the Hunting Dogs; *Eridanus, Fornax, Canes Venatici.* The Lion, the Wolf, the Southern Cross; *Leo, Lupus, Crux*—but without the naked sky above him, the words seemed nothing but mute and meaningless shapes dying into white. Only the stars themselves could give them life.

He was standing in the darkness by the small window when Paweł came into the room just before curfew. Gracian did not move. He felt Paweł regard him for a time in silence and then take off his coat and boots and lie on his bed. The brothers did not speak. For a long while there was no sound or movement between them. Then Paweł said, "You can always watch from there."

Gracian stood where he was, his face cooled by the glass. "It's not the same," he said.

He listened to the sound of Paweł breathing and the wind whipping through the crab-apple tree, sending slow languid ripples across the black lour of forest beyond.

"Please understand, Gracian," Paweł said. "It's different now. There is danger out there, and you're too young for it. Please—have some sense."

Silence, and then words.

"But it's fine for *you?*" said the boy.

"Gracian." Paweł's face was soft, pleading.

There was no answer.

When Paweł next spoke his voice was firm. "It would do you good to be scared, brother," he said. "There is much to be scared of, down here in Poland. I will be staying with the Malewskas for some nights, but don't think that lets you off. I'll be watching you, boy."

Gracian heard Paweł's body shifting the springs. He did not doubt his brother's words. His eyes lifted up into the beyond and he stood there with his hands in his pockets while behind him Paweł stared unsleeping at nothing and the wind didn't stop.

✦

A month passed and the snows came.

It was November of 1940. For four weeks he had been unable to risk his skin to look at the sky. The snow clung to every surface it could and was drawn into a fine top mist by the wind, and the time had come for Old Man Morek to sit outside his house and play his sad songs to the winter mornings. No one knew how old Old Man Morek was, though the children gossiped and whispered to each other that he had lived beyond one hundred, two hundred; he could not die. His long face was etched with a labyrinth of lines, as if his skin were a lake that retained the surface impressions of an age of rainstorms. He too had once been a miner.

Each morning when the snows came, Old Man Morek would sit upon the crumbling step of his house, his frail body secreted within a mound of coats and wrappings of wool, fur, and cracked leather. Warmed this way, he would sing unaccompanied to whoever would listen, or to no one perhaps, in a voice unexpectedly clear and deep and sonorous. Old Polish folk tunes, laments of the Turning Earth and the Passing of Time and the Endlessness of Labour and the Withering of Flowers.

Nobody disturbed Old Man Morek's performances. Even the special police seemed to accept him as a part of the landscape.

Each morning on his way to colliery Richter, Gracian would nod his greeting to the old man. The old man would incline his head in acknowledgement, and the echoes of his song would reach the boy as he passed and merge with the substance of some well of feeling within him. It was not anger or frustration that had overcome Gracian, but melancholy. The world had become dull and formless. Every day became the same slow parade of undifferentiated shapes and actions. Like a ship, he sailed by the stars. Without them he was lost.

In the mines, deep down beneath the earth's surface, was the worst time. He worked with Gerard Dylong and half listened to his partner's latest theories of where the sulphur might lie and to his stories of how the village was before, when he was a child and Poland did not exist, when the language of his forefathers had to be learned from their mouths for it was not to be found in schoolbooks, when there was nothing to see but fields and farms. Dylong was the greatest spinner of tales, Gracian thought, in all the world.

Sometimes the coal glistened like a frozen black ocean. Other times they came across prehistoric fossils, imprinted like transparencies in the rock: strange animals; giant leaves, with veins like aerial maps of all Poland, displayed one on top of another.

Gracian worked with his mind inert and his muscles moving as if by some independent impulse. The work was always hard and unrelenting and left him dirtied by an indelible film of coal. Sensing the boy's quiet and his depression, Gerard Dylong became gruff and would often try to goad him into speech. When this failed he would slap him and force him to work harder, shouting, "Silesia is nothing but one giant lump of coal, boy! Somewhere inside there's treasure! Dig harder! Dig!" And Gracian would fall deeper into his waking slumber until shift end and the rising of the lifts into day.

In the village of Maleńkowice, too, there were stories, stories hushed and murmured and spread only in the most private of conversations. Stories, tales, whispers: of more villagers taken from the street or from their homes or from their beds and loaded onto trains and army trucks to Germany; of men beaten for refusing or being unable to speak German to officials; of informants and special favours and old friends become bitter and unspeaking; and of the Jews. There had only ever been five or six Jewish families in Maleńkowice, but one month before the invasion they had simply disappeared. No one knew of their fate. Some claimed they had settled in Romania or Hungary, others that they had died or been captured midjourney. Many Jews from surrounding parts had been taken to live packed up together like farm animals in a town to the east called Sosnowiec. Gracian had heard from Dylong that they were building a work camp up in Oświęcim, sixty kilometres southeast of Katowice.

It seemed to Gracian that the stories were like a disease. He had seen them infect the whole village. He had seen them infect his family and transform his mother's face into something grey and withdrawn. Now when he was not suspecting she would wave her spoon at him and tell him to keep quiet and take care, and Gracian would tell her he understood—though in fact he understood little. There were days when the boy felt the stories humming in the frozen air, spoken not through voices but through secret glances exchanged in the street, looks of fear and suspicion and distrust shot between those who had lived together for many years as neighbours. Days when, Gracian thought, the very air sang and trembled with the tension of the unsaid, and the only rest from it all seemed to come when, at some undisclosed time of day—on his way to or from work, perhaps, or with his mother buying food—a German carrier truck, its dark load unseen, rumbled through the cobbled main street, disturbing the grit. Then those around would stop and watch it pass before them, the snow swirling wildly in its wake, heading, ever unstopping, toward a destination unknown.

His days were busy, his mother and Francesca were always occupied with their labours, and Gracian felt himself craving the company of his brother. He was aching to speak to Paweł, to impart something to him he could not himself define, and to find a steadiness and a mooring in his brother's words. But Paweł was absent more than ever before. He would appear only occasionally in the house, and then he would argue with their mother and afterward become still and wordless. Sometimes he would bring Anna Malewska with him, and at these times, looking upon her, watching her move, Gracian would feel his cheeks grow hot and red and he would become awkward in his actions and have to leave, hurrying for the coolness of his room.

The rations were not enough to feed them. A week's worth of bread, milk, sausage meat, and eggs could be finished within three days. "How are we supposed to live like this?" Gracian's mother said. "With a mother, a baby, a husband, and two strong boys to feed!" Despite his habitual absence and the tension ever increasing between them, she still considered Paweł a household member. "It's impossible, I tell you. Impossible!"

Gracian's mother had grown up in the country, in a collection of houses that passed as a village named Pietraszowice. She still had many friends there. In the country, where life was lived off the land, food was a little more plentiful but the farmers were desperate for other supplies: fabric, kitchenware, sewing needles. Thus, without fuss or debate, as if some binding resolution had been quietly made, Gracian's mother began to visit the place of her birth.

On early-shift days, Gracian accompanied her after work. Together, braced against the cold and with his mother dressed in the old way, the way of the country, in long skirt and heavy tunic, they would walk through the village to the station. There they showed their identification to the armed guards and stood on the stretch of platform where the snow was doused with salt to await the local train. Eventually it would come, loud and steaming, and idle before them. It was sixty-five kilometres to their destination. The journey took one hour and thirty-five minutes. Gracian sat with his hands in his lap and watched the dull scrub by the tracks give way swiftly to flat open country, the snow thick, dense, virginal, halted only by the horizon line, as if severed by the grey weight of the lowering sky. At Pawonków station they disembarked.

From there it was another mile to Pietraszowice. They walked, feet crumpling the snow, among clogged paths made not of cobblestones but of flattened dirt, and the boy held his mother's elbow when the going was hard. As they walked, Gracian looked around at the pure white inclines surrounding him and remembered how, when he was a child, he would take the wooden sled his father made and spend the day skidding down the gentle hills. A time that had passed. He was fifteen years of age. No age for sledding, or the joy of snow.

When they reached the farming settlement they headed for the heat of the first house, that of Jan Piowcyk and his wife and their five children, and then progressed to the others. They were greeted warmly but their hosts always seemed tired, and there was about the proceedings the guardedness of business. After Gracian's mother had exchanged pleasantries, she removed the bundle of cloth from her tunic and opened it out upon the table. When she did this, Gracian noticed, her movements were delicate, considered, like a doctor's. Then the host brought out food—smoked ham, meats of many kinds, eggs, milk— and placed it opposite his mother's offering.

After a deal was struck they never lingered.

"I am very lucky," his mother would say. "Lucky to have old friends like you. God has been kind to me."

"We, too, are lucky. You know we trust you. Everything is difficult, now the fields are dead under the snow," they would reply.

Gracian's mother was a thin woman, even bony, her chest flat and her hips narrow. But returning from Pietraszo-wice she would be fat, buxom, swollen with health. In the lining of her skirt and tunic she had fashioned pouches, and in the pouches she tucked the food pressed tight against her underclothes. She became a walking pantry. Her breasts were two proud joints of ham, her potbelly filled out with a stoppered jug of milk and other fresh dairy products, her arms plumped invitingly with sausage coils, her cheeks flushed under the weight of it all. Transformed thus, she would keep her son close to her on their return as she waddled through the slush, Gracian's hands ready to rectify any slippage of her ballast until they

reached Pawonków. His job upon arrival both at Pawonków station and Maleńkowice station was always to direct
them both away from guards who might have noticed
them upon their outward trip and to tend his mother as
she moved, as if she were pregnant or decrepit. When
they reached the village they did not take the main street
to the house but hurried through back lanes on a cir-
cuitous route that took them home in twice the time it
should have taken. But still they had their food.

Two times, they were caught, the first at Maleńkowice,
the second at Pawonków.

In Maleńkowice there had been a young tall set-faced
guard with thick brown stubble around his underjaw.
This was to be a random search.

"Stop, old lady," he said in German as they passed him.
"Wait there."

Gracian's stomach dipped and rose. He felt his hair
bristle. Before either could react, the guard had upended
his rifle and slung it behind his back and was reaching out
to frisk his mother. She slapped his hand away, affronted.
She could speak German, as could Gracian.

"How dare you!" she hollered. "How dare you touch
me! An old woman with a bad back and swollen legs!"

The soldier smiled a tight smile, his eyes flickering.
"Stay still," he said. "Come on, lady."

She began to brush his hands away, slapping, resisting.
"I don't believe it!" Her voice was loud, almost screaming.
"Abuse! Abuse! You wish to abuse an old widow who
needs her son to guide her. A scandal!"

Gracian could not move. The soldier had begun to blink rapidly. His face was becoming the color of a rash. "Stay *still*!" he said.

"Scandal! Pervert!" she continued. "Rape! This is rape! The rape of an old woman! This man here is a pervert!"

They were causing an obstruction. People were bustling behind them, past them, muttering, looking, passing and passing. The next train was thundering in at the platform edge, the steam plume gusting. Further down the platform, two other guards had been alerted by the noise, and the nearer flicked a cigarette stub onto the tracks and began to wander slowly toward them. The young guard looked over at him, uneasy. Gracian's mother kept shouting.

"Abuse! Help me!"

"Fine!" the guard said suddenly. "Go! Get away from me! Go, you mad old bitch! Go!"

They went.

But it was the second time, the chance that never should have been granted them, that lingered in Gracian's mind. It came back often, puzzling, disquieting him.

It occurred at Pawonków station. A busy afternoon, busier than usual. A small tight crowd waiting for the train, pushing against one another at the identification checkpoint. Gracian was surprised by the people, the hustle of forms, and did not see the guard waiting some distance from the checkpoint, the guard who had watched them arrive. The boy led his mother straight toward him. The guard was older, thickset, untidy. As soon as he saw the boy and the woman he hoisted up his rifle and stopped

Gracian's mother short, the muzzle pressing in against her heart.

A tiny noise, an exhalation, escaped her throat. Seeing her like that, Gracian felt a knife blade at his throat. This time, he thought. This time for sure.

The guard looked them both up and down. He kept the rifle where it was with one hand and with his other pulled a cigarette from his top pocket and then a lighter. He lit the cigarette, and a cloud of smoke billowed from his lips.

"Gained some weight, haven't we?" he said in German through the smoke. "Must be that country air. Is that what it is?"

Gracian's mother opened her mouth and then closed it. Gracian realized he was shaking.

"Or maybe the bun's in the oven. Just like that. *Bang!* And the sprog's shown up." He laughed once, a staccato wheeze.

There was a silence.

"The boy's not with me," Gracian's mother said softly. And then, "What will you do?"

The guard looked at them both. His gaze was hard, scouring. "Don't miss your train," he said then, almost casually, lowering the gun.

Gracian's mother stared at the guard. Then she moved slowly to her left, her eyes upon his. She caught hold of Gracian's cuff and pulled him with her and began to jog and then run to the platform. Of the two, only Gracian looked back.

The look in his eyes. A thin electric cord between them, vanished now in the curl of smoke.

"Why didn't he arrest us, Mother?" he said breathlessly.

She shot him a glance. There was sweat on her forehead. "*Because,* boy. Don't ask such questions," she said, hurrying along.

The next week they made the same journey. The guard was nowhere to be seen.

And so it was. The snow had erased all traces of summer. The yellow air of the hot months, the blooming forest, the rich green pastures, all had become as unfamiliar as the phrases of a dead language.

Each and every night, Gracian stood by his window and looked upon what was lost to him.

The days went on: the turning earth, the withering of flowers.

One night that month Gracian had a dream. He dreamt he was back amid the mud and grass in the viewing place, but he had forgotten the magnifying glass. He scrabbled in his pockets for it awhile and then finally gave up and sat back, his arms outstretched behind him. His eyes rested then, as they often did, upon the brightest of the stars, the pole star. It seemed brighter than ever. It pulsed and shimmered and its light was of a whiteness and a purity that Gracian would never have guessed could be possible and its brightness sighed like the giant breaths of some Creature of Light.

Frustrated that he could not examine the star through

the convex glass, Gracian squinted, channelling his concentration to the front of his head and feeling the dull pressure behind the holes in his skull. And as he watched, the star grew. He kept staring hard and the star kept growing. It grew larger and still larger until Gracian could see its blue aura like a gas flame playing about the pure white globe. It was not simply growing but coming closer.

And now the star was pressing against the forest roof, the bright noiseless curve of a new horizon. And still it came, until it was bending flat the distant rim of trees, snapping them like kindling, and its belly was only a foot now from Gracian's upturned face. Gracian paused and then reached out his hand to touch it. Its thin blue atmosphere brought with it a gentle breeze, lapping his skin. The texture of the surface was firm but yielding, like rubber. The breeze ruffled his hair and the light was gentle, ebbing. Gracian was not afraid.

Then he noticed that a series of white rungs protruded from the star face. As his eyes grew accustomed to the magnesium glare he saw more of them, rungs one after another stretching up the curvature of the star to the vanishing crest. He reached for one and curled his hand around it and felt a lifting, a sucking, and his legs flew from beneath him and his feet were on another rung and he was hanging upside down above the earth.

With little effort he started to climb. He felt at rest and at peace and he was happy. He climbed the curve a short distance and then he felt the great star shudder and there was a rustling and creaking of wood as the star began to rise.

It rose higher and higher above the forest and, looking down now, he could see the whole of Maleńkowice below: the fields; the forking stretch of streets and houses, including his own; the grey hulk of the mines. Gracian climbed and the star rose until he was at the very top, his ankles brushed by pale blue shadow, and the village was nothing but an ideogram scrawled across the land.

Gracian looked around him. There were many other stars suspended in the thick black night, a galaxy-ful. Seeing them, Gracian felt a surge of warmth that spread from his heart in waves. He walked about on the star surface, craning his neck at the panorama, and then he noticed that a cluster of stars to his right seemed to be moving. As he watched, the stars slid out of their positions and jostled and slid again, passing each other and aligning and realigning. Gracian realized that they were gathering into shapes of light against the black. Letters. Words. They were sky-spelling.

LOOK CLOSER

they read.

And Gracian felt a shift, a change, and turned around and saw Paweł standing some feet away from him with Anna Malewska. He regarded them for a time, and then Anna stepped forward beyond Paweł. Her eyes were dark and depthless and her hair kissed her face, and her lips were parted in a smile like no other. She lifted a hand and gestured to him, once.

Gracian turned back to where the letters had been, but the stars had moved. Now they formed an endless chain of stepping stars, stretching into the far-off emptiness; the closest star was near enough for Gracian to step onto.

He turned back, and now with Paweł and Anna Malewska stood his father and Gerard Dylong, and each of them looked at him in turn. Their eyes were knowing. Uncertain which way to move—toward the knowledge of the faces or the mystery of the stars—Gracian closed his eyes and held his breath and then, in a burst of spontaneous motion, he spun away from Paweł and Anna Malewska and his father and Gerard Dylong and jumped forward into the night. The stars had gone and the night had become a sheer vortex of solid coal and as he fell his hands scraped against it, a crumbling rain of black sooting his face, and his feet scrabbled to gain purchase, but there was nowhere to go but headlong into the convulsion of his chest and the snapping open of his eyes to the morning.

Paweł was home. When Gracian came back from the colliery he was sunk down in a chair in the kitchen under the bare yellow bulb with his boots up on a chair. He was tapping the good fingers of his crippled hand against the tabletop and then rubbing the wood in little strokes and then tapping again. He was listening to his mother, his face shadowed, lowered. She was standing at the opposite end of the table, leaning on it with both hands, talking with her back bent and her face jutting out toward Paweł. Gracian regarded them from the doorway and then shivered in the warmth of the room and took off his coat and hat, the snow flecks falling away and dying tiny liquid deaths on the floorboards.

No one acknowledged him.

"It can't go on, Paweł," his mother was saying. "There

isn't enough of anything. This morning they took the animals. Pig, the hens. Gone. Something has to—"

"Mother, I've told you," Paweł said.

She lifted her arm abruptly in a stiff movement, her finger pointing to silence him. An oil-slick shadow swept across the table, remained.

The door opened. Francesca's husband, Józef Kukła, came into the room. He was a tall and silent man, with a thin sculptured face. He was an irritable man too, with a tendency to work himself into a fury. Many times Gracian had heard his arguments with Francesca rising up through the house.

He was tapping out his pipe and pressing in the tobacco and toying with it in his hand. He did not like Paweł. In the young man's absence, Kukła had often cursed his name. He walked to the sink and poured some water and stood and regarded the pair, the pipe bulb cupped in his palm. He smiled in a way that made clear he would not be leaving.

"Go away, Józef. Please," Gracian's mother said.

Kukła lifted the pipe and put it tenderly between his lips and lit up, puffing. He looked at Paweł and Paweł ignored him.

"Mother." Paweł spoke evenly, quietly. "No one will employ me. Not because of my hand or my health. Because I was in the Polish army, yes. And because I am an outsider here and always have been. Now is no time to trust outsiders, they think. Now is no time for trust at all."

"But it's too *much*." Her voice rose a tone. "Have you *tried*? Can you at least tell me that? All this time have you really been looking?"

The question extended across the table and faded. The time for Paweł to answer came and passed. He looked at his boot tops and lifted a hand and dragged it across his chin. At the door Gracian felt a pulling inside him, a sinking.

"Why must it always be your way, Mother? Your way or nothing," Paweł said finally.

"He's a lout. A lazy good-for-nothing," said Józef Kukła now, his voice a sudden intrusion into the balance of the room.

"Quiet, Józef," she said softly, looking now at her hands, the splayed fingers. "Leave here. This is between my son and me."

Paweł lifted his head and the shadows on his face fell away.

"Mother, you can't understand my life now. The way I live. The choices I have made. There have been choices made, Mother, and not just by me—"

"Yes," said Józef Kukła. "You have chosen to laze around like a dog. You have chosen to put a strain on your mother, your sister, to put your whole family at risk. No, I will not leave. It's time for you to behave decently, like a man should."

Kukła's eyes were molten brown. The pipe was shaking in his hand; the thin smoke stream shattered, whirling.

Paweł sat up slowly, as if moving each muscle one by one. He pulled his boots off the chair and placed them upon the floorboards.

At the door Gracian could not move; he felt he was at the edge of a great abyss. He could not move, he could not move.

A noise escaped his mother like a sob. "Paweł!" she said. "Why can't you see? We are all afraid! Why do you want to die?"

"But you smuggle food!" Paweł shouted, standing up now, his hands in fists.

"*You* speak to me of smuggling?" she scoffed, her head cocked. "I do it out of necessity! Necessity! To feed my children!"

"Don't preach to me about necessity!"

She threw her hands up to her face. "I lost your father. Why have you always been intent on making me lose a son?"

"My father?" Paweł said. "*Disease* killed my father. This village killed my father. The coal in the air killed my father, ate him up from inside. I *know* what killed him, Mother. In the end it will kill us all."

"That's enough!" Józef Kukła stepped forward, reaching out toward Paweł, the pipe under his whitened knuckles now suddenly toylike, ridiculous.

And then Paweł turning, finally meeting his eyes and not as tall as Kukła but a stronger animal and pulling back his arm and driving it into Kukła's stomach. Kukła wheezing, one leg skipping back to retain balance, and Paweł rounding on him, bringing down another punch, but Kukła fast and, flinging his arms up around Paweł's waist, gripping hard, his red cheek pushed in against Paweł's stomach, forcing him back four or five paces, slammed hard up against the wall, and the bare bulb swinging wild veering shadows. Paweł was blinking rapidly, winded now but bringing up his knee with force, and Kukła's grip slackening and Paweł heaving one sharp punch into the face and blood now visible on Kukła's lips. Then both men were down on the floor, wrestling, no words but only noises in the rising dust.

Kukła had dropped his pipe. Gracian watched it. The tobacco burned. The smoke cast a shadow. He could smell it.

And now his mother was yelling, no words but only noises—*"Haaaa! Haaaa!"*—dancing around the two men, shaking her hands and brushing her fingers against them and slipping off them, repelled, as if the two men had become one liquid mass; and the door slammed open once more and Francesca rushed in, her eyes wide and unbelieving and the baby crying in her arms, wailing, its tiny face raw and crumpled, and Francesca setting the baby on the tabletop and moving over to help her mother. And finally Paweł was dragged up, breathless, panting, his neck veins throbbing, and Kukła rolling on the floor covering his eyes with his palms, and Paweł's hair smeared against his forehead, no blood on his face but dark reddened blotches. And his mother shouting.

"Out! Out! Out! Out! Out! Get out of here! *Haaa! You are not welcome in this house!*"

Paweł sniffed and pushed his damp hair back and snatched his coat and hat. Without speaking, he walked past the table across the room and to the door. He did not look at Gracian. He opened the door onto a rectangle of frozen white. Outside, the snow was still falling, and he stepped into it.

Gracian watched him go. He felt despair. He felt it as a candle flame, starting at his feet and rising up to ignite his body until his heart burned and his eyes stung and a choking pressure in his throat caused him to gasp out, a gasp that crippled him, bending him at the waist. *"Paweł!"*

From where he was now, in the street, in the snow, Paweł stopped and turned and saw Gracian. He stood for a few moments and raised one hand. Then he turned back again into the blank white afternoon and was soon gone, and Gracian felt suddenly certain that he would never see his brother again.

Later, as Francesca tried to nurse Józef Kukła, who would not stop cursing, Gracian's mother stood and came over to Gracian and looked her son in the eyes and embraced him and refused to let go.

"Secrets, nothing but secrets," she said in a low voice, close to his ear, almost whispering. Then she looked steadily at the boy's face. "You don't have secrets, do you, Gracian? Not like your reckless brother. You wouldn't keep secrets from me? At least not big ones?"

Gracian not struggling, but thinking it best to yield to his mother's arms, and shaking his head no, rested his cheek on the cleft of her shoulder which was shaking gently now, and remembered.

Eleven years old. The black shape of a man filling the yellow doorway. *Perhaps now you'll have a hobby,* the book spinning from his hand down onto the mattress.

The constellation of his birth was Gemini. *Wstęp Do Astronomii* had shown him; fifteen stars formed its main body, and the two largest in the diagram signified the heads of twin brothers. Their names were Castor and Pollux. They were born from an egg, for their mother was a swan; each had a different father. It was said that Pollux was the son of a god and immortal but that Castor was human and could perish. In their lifetimes Castor became famous as a rider of horses, and Pollux fought and won many battles. The brothers had power together over winds and sea. When Castor was killed by his cousin, Pollux begged the gods to let him die with his brother, for in his heart he had only abiding love for him. The gods listened to his pleas, and finally the twins were etched together in the heavens, their hands bearing spears aloft.

Fifteen stars. It had seemed amazing to Gracian how something so simple could make for such a story. That was the marvel of it—from points of light, whole destinies might unfurl.

✦

A week passed without a sign of Paweł. No one in the house spoke of the argument. Only the bruises on the face of Józef Kukła acknowledged its occurrence, and those too were fading.

In the village, Old Man Morek kept his vigil, his hats and coats a livery of snowflakes. He had begun to sing a new song, a song Gracian had never before heard him sing. It boomed and lilted endlessly on the bitter wind. It was about the mountain people.

> *Góralu, czy ci nie żal,*
> *odchodić od stron ojczystych,*
> *świerkowych lasów i hal,*
> *i tych potoków srebrzystych?*
> *Góralu! Czy ci nie żal,*

Góralu! wracaj do hal.
Highlander, aren't you regretful
for leaving your homeland,
the forests of pine and the meadows,
the silver mountain streams?
Highlander! Aren't you regretful?
Highlander! Turn back to your green meadows.

Gracian mined each day from 6 A.M. to 2 P.M., seven and a half straight hours with one half-hour break. He lost himself in the work. With Gerard Dylong he could load eight or nine wagons over the twenty-wagon quota. There were no days off.

"Well, well, Galileo," Dylong would say, watching the boy work as if there were not an end to his endurance. "Finally becoming a man?"

Always Dylong told him aimless, rambling stories of the old Silesia. Always they found no sulphur. Always they smoked a cigarette together after their shift. For Gracian, there was nothing but this daily ritual.

At the end of the week, Gracian passed out into the day after finishing and crossed the courtyard, where men walked quickly or lingered for a time, talking in the cold. His body ached with the work. He looked at his feet as he went, his mind empty. In his right hand he held the carbide lamp, which he kept always at home with him. Despite having showered, he felt the coal dust still on his skin, clinging like sweat. He felt the hardness of his arms and shoulders, the tautness of sinew. Approaching the wire-mesh perimeter fence, he glanced up.

Beneath the battered metal sign that read RICHTER

stood Paweł. He was leaning against the gate edge with his hands dug into his coat pockets and his hat pulled down, breathing white. Gracian stopped and closed his eyes and counted to five and then opened them and found Paweł still standing there in the winter glare.

"Hello, Gracian," Paweł said.

Gracian gave a flick of his hand by way of greeting. He looked at his brother. There was some swelling on his cheek.

"How is Mother?" Paweł said.

Again he simply gestured. No words would come to him.

Paweł cleared his throat and squinted into the sky above Gracian's head and then looked at the ground.

"Blasted cold," he said, as if to himself. Then he looked at Gracian. "There is work down at colliery Osok. In two days' time I will see the foreman. I need someone who can speak German. To translate," he said.

Like many other villagers born in the early years of independence, Paweł had never learned German. Gracian had learned mostly from his mother, but Paweł was never one to listen hard to the teachings of others.

Gracian continued looking at Paweł. He examined his face and saw a strange expression in his eyes. Eventually he spoke.

"I'll come," he said.

It was December 1940. The snows showed no sign of abating.

Two days later, after his shift, Gracian walked through the snow to the Malewskas' flat. The flat was owned by the mining company. It was small and saw little light. The walls were the green of damp earth.

When he arrived, there was only Anna. Her voice told him to come in and he pushed open the door and saw her standing with her back to him, framed in the doorway of the tiny kitchen. She was engaged in some task: drying crockery, perhaps. Her black silken hair was pulled back and tied with a thin length of red cloth.

"Sit down, Gracian," she said, without turning.

Gracian took his hat off and sat on one of the wooden chairs. In Anna's unobserving presence he felt aware of the details of his own body: the largeness of his hands, the gestures of his arms, the heavy, mechanical movements of his legs. Already he felt the heat growing in his cheeks and temples. He sat still and stared at the matted fur of his hat.

Anna came in now with a mug of coffee, saying, "You must be tired." He reached up and took it, keeping his eyes lowered and feeling the coolness of her fingers in the exchange. He took a sip. Between the hem of her long skirt and the rim of her leather slippers he could see her bare ankles. He watched them move across the room and saw her sit opposite him and watched the ankles cross over each other lightly, feet heels-up on the worn tan carpet.

"Paweł is just coming. He's getting dressed," she said.

Gracian looked up then and met her eyes and saw she was smiling in a way he thought suggested puzzlement. Her face had a radiance that Gracian thought could make even time stop to look in its direction.

"And how is young Gracian?" she said.

He drank again from the mug. The coffee fumes bathed his face. "Fine," he said. And then, "I'm fifteen," his eyes averted.

Anna smiled. They sat together there for a time in silence.

There was a noise then, a loud shuffling, and Paweł came in through a door Gracian had not noticed. He was wearing old suit trousers, a pale shirt and a brown sweater and over that a woollen jacket. He was newly shaven, red about the ears and throat. He seemed agitated, alert. He was tugging at the points of his shirt collar, folding them down and smoothing them over the neckline of his sweater.

He placed his good hand on Anna's shoulder and she tilted her head slightly and reached up to brush his knuckles and then with her fingers reached back to feel the smooth black knot of hair, her movements quick and tender, probing.

"Gracian! Good!" Paweł said passionately, his face animated. "Are you ready? It'll be a long walk and a cold one. We need something to warm us, I think. Anna, will you fetch us something to warm our hearts?"

Gracian had never heard Paweł speak like this, with such abandon. In his mind he tried to fit the words to Paweł or Paweł to the words but could accomplish neither. He was not enjoying his stay here. He was filled with the wariness of the trespasser and wanted only to leave.

Anna shook her head and laughed and then stood. Paweł sat down heavily in her place and rubbed his hands together and grinned at Gracian. Anna returned with a half-full bottle of rye vodka and two clean shot glasses. She filled them, handed them over, and stood with her hands upon her hips.

"Drink!" Paweł said.

Gracian looked at the crystal liquid in his hand and then raised the glass to his mouth. They drained their glasses together. Gracian gagged once, then felt the seeping flame in his throat.

Paweł clapped his hands together and stood. They put on their coats and fastened them and tied their hats close under their chins, then gloves and woollen scarves. Gracian led the way to the door. He heard Paweł say, "I'll be back soon," and turned and saw Paweł and Anna embrace. She slid her arms around the bulk of his coat, and he placed his hand on her cheek. They kissed on the mouth, and when they parted both seemed struck with a sadness.

Looking at them like this, Gracian felt as if he were invisible; he had become nothing but a frame containing this image of his brother and Anna Malewska collected between the dull walls. And as an image yields up only its surface, so Gracian understood then that an impenetrable wall encased and sealed them both and held them safe from all enquiry.

It was over four kilometres to colliery Osok. The wind had picked up, and in it the snow did not fall but sucked and circulated in shifting rhythms. It clung lightly but persistently to everything, until the walking figures seemed built of snow: concentrations of white moving in the haze. They were heading northeastward, faces into the wind, and if they had tried to talk—which they did not—their voices would have been swept up and lost completely.

Soon they left the narrow outskirts and were on a country lane where the white was thicker and unbroken and great banks of it sat upon the lane edges. As they passed, it would occasionally slide and collapse and re-form itself, locked in the private geologies of snow. On the path they were utterly alone. They met no one. They walked with their backs bent and their hands pressing their collars against their cheeks. The path was straight and unrelenting.

They stopped once for Gracian to wrap his scarf tighter in a wadded loop about his chin. Paweł grappled with his own hat straps, hands clumsy in their gloves, and retied them firm. Gracian squinted into grey and saw there was no distinction now between earth and sky. They seemed in neither day nor night but rather in a lost and in-between time, a single moment extended out for-ever. Gracian longed for the mist to part before him and reveal the special clarity of a darkened sky. And as he longed, it seemed to him that the stars he could not see were also certainty; they were all the certainty of the universe gathered and condensed and sharpened until the black night was punctured a billion times and the light of eternity shone through, bright and clear and unwavering.

"We're over halfway!" Paweł shouted hoarsely into the whirling snow, gesturing at his brother to continue.

Gracian had never felt such cold. He thought their journey would not end.

Then through it came the first houses of Osok. Two Ger-man guards sat hunched and shivering in a small wooden signal shack, their rifles drawn up against them and held by the barrels, but the brothers passed without question. Between the snow-washed shadows of houses the wind retracted its needle claws.

The village of Osok existed only as a bare and tiny annex to its colliery. Its mines were ancillary, smaller than those of colliery Richter, and it was for this reason perhaps that its nameplate had not been Germanized. The colliery building was brown-brick solid and without embellishment and towered up as if it had sprung directly from the rock from which it had for so long drawn its means of business. Reaching it, the brothers crossed the forecourt and found the offices and the door marked FOREMAN, gold on glass.

Paweł paused with his glove upon the doorknob. He inhaled deeply and stared at his hand. Here beneath the heavy unassuming cornice of the entrance the storm could not reach them, and though the cold hung round like a living thing there was the quietude of a kind of shelter.

Gracian looked carefully at his brother, at his pausing, and felt the time was right to ask a question that for two days he had not dared ask. The words before had seemed dangerous to him, full of deadly weight; it was as if their voicing might tip some invisible scale and plunge the world into terror. But now in his brother's pausing, and in the reality of the bricks and the ending of the journey, a hole had opened to claim the words, and there was no terror.

"Why, Paweł?" he said. "Why did you decide to come?"

Paweł looked up, his mouth open slightly in surprise, as if he had been woken from a doze. Gracian watched as once more his features hardened, re-formed to composure.

Until there was not a hint of anything behind Paweł's eyes.

"Mother was right about one thing," he said. "It's safer for me to work."

He swung open the door and stepped inside.

They waited for a time in a dim-lit room where a secretary took their names, thumbed through a leather-bound book, found something, and snapped the book shut again. She told them to hang up their coats and wait. She looked ill, Gracian thought, as if she had not been sleeping. Then the wooden box on her desk made a sound and she pointed to the misted glass of the second door. Paweł patted Gracian lightly on the back and they went through.

A wide desk was the only furniture in the room, save the chairs on which two men sat and one empty chair on the opposite side of the desk. The plaster on the walls was fissured and peeling. Two electric fan heaters stood by two of the walls and were humming softly; the air there in the room was much too hot and smelled stale. A third man leaned loosely against the wall with his right shoe sole flat behind him, smoking a cigarette slowly, looking at the smoke as it rose. One of the men at the desk was absorbed in reading a broadsheet German newspaper with his face tense in concentration; the other, older and heavier than the others, was looking intently at Paweł and Gracian, his hands clasped before him. He was smiling in a way that seemed neither friendly nor very hostile. He had about him the air of one who could not be surprised or moved beyond his own compulsions. His hands were thick and looked dusty.

"Herr Sófka," this man now said. *"Bitte."* He raised one of his hands and directed it toward the empty chair. Paweł moved round and sat down, his body too large for the seat. Gracian stood behind him, keeping his arms by his sides. Paweł coughed and fingered the buttonholes of his jacket.

Gracian noticed suddenly that one of the men, the one at the wall, was familiar to him, a German who had lived in Maleńkowice when Gracian was a child. His name was Albert Schwabe. He had owned a shop; Gracian remembered trips there with his mother. Paweł, he remembered too, had once been on good terms with Schwabe and would nod to him in the street if they passed. But neither Paweł nor Schwabe showed any signs now of recognition or of acknowledgement. Both kept their eyes locked steady— Paweł's on the far wall and Schwabe's on his cigarette, its slow burning, the vertical smoke line rising.

The foreman transferred his gaze to Gracian. In German he asked if he were here to translate and Gracian answered that he was and added, "But my speaking is not perfect."

"Don't worry, boy, we'll keep it simple," he said, and then glanced at Paweł and lifted both hands and smoothed them down the seams of his trouser legs beneath the desk. The heaters hummed like insects.

"Well, Mr. Sófka, you want work here, is that right?" the foreman said, and Gracian translated.

"I need work. I am willing to work for you," Paweł said, and then Gracian.

"And why are you not working already? Those who have not been working are usually troublemakers. There is no place for troublemakers. Or rather there are special places. Are you a troublemaker, Mr. Sófka?"

In his translation Gracian made himself like a glass mirror. He made himself feel no store in the words being spoken, as if they were simply packages wrapped for delivery and his job was to take the place of deliveryman, and though a part of his mind felt restive he stamped that part down and kept it safely away.

"I need work. I will work hard for you," Paweł said.

The man gave a nod that was less a nod than a lowering of his chin toward his loosened necktie. Then, with his head down, he glanced over at the newspaper man, but the newspaper man turned a page with a rustling and kept reading. The man set his eyes straight again at Paweł.

"I see you have an injury. Tell me, how did you get it? How do you expect to work the mines with a useless hand?"

The man asked and then Gracian asked. It was so hot in the room, the air stifling. Sweat ran from his armpits and over his ribs.

"An accident in childhood; fell under a horse. It's not useless. I can hold an axe or shovel better than many men can."

The man frowned and consulted a sheaf of paper he had all the while before him, but the consulting seemed more show than real.

"It says in this file that you were in the Polish army, although it doesn't explain why you are now here looking for a job. It also says you once spent some time in prison. The injury was not given you in either of these places?"

Gracian hesitated. He had never heard of Paweł being in prison. He did not know what this meant or would mean or even if it was true. He wiped the sweat from his brow and neck and looked at the foreman, and the foreman looked expectantly at him and he translated.

"No," Paweł said after a moment. Gracian saw that his brother's face was flushed in the heat, but his body remained stationary and he did not look at Gracian.

The man gave a loud exhalation as if he were deflating and leaned far back in his chair. He dragged one of his slab hands over his hair and looked from Paweł to Gracian and back to Paweł again with a quizzical expression. Then suddenly he moved forward and extended a finger at Gracian.

"Translate," he said. "Every word."

The German looked hard at Paweł and spoke.

"Before you go, Mr. Sófka, let me ask you one question. What do you think of the way things are here? In your homeland. The situation. What are your views on these things?"

Gracian translated. Paweł shifted in his seat. For the first time he seemed unsure of himself and of what his choice of words might now be.

"I am a Pole," Paweł said then. "I feel what my countrymen feel."

The man raised his eyebrows theatrically, the pale wide forehead creasing. "Ah. A Pole. A Pole. Well, that is certainly an interesting proposition"—the man heard Gracian falter and glanced sharply at him—"that's *idea,* boy, you may say *idea*"—and Gracian said the word as he had been asked, and the man continued. "And I wonder why it is you call yourself a Pole, Mr. Sófka. Let me tell you about your *countrymen,* Mr. Sófka. Your countrymen are called Silesians and your countrymen do not exist. Historically they have not existed, for they inhabited a nation so weak and confused in itself as not to exist. They have always been nothing but vessels—empty glasses—for the filling and discarding of others. This is an orphan country you come from, Mr. Sófka. A tiny orphan child of a place. How do you say it—a *sierota*? After the war the smallest part of you was robbed from us. But now we have you as well.

"You were never Polish, you see. Not a Pole. You were confused, a nothing. And now you are a German. We have taken complete custody. No more problem, no more confusion. We have come to reclaim you like the father you never had. And you are lucky to have our acceptance, Mr. Sófka. You will learn in time to see the truth of this. For your own sake you will learn it."

He eased himself back again and crossed his arms and brushed his chin with his thumb.

"What is your response, Mr. Sófka?" he said then, with his eyebrows winched up in that same way.

Gracian expected his brother to stand, but he did not. He did not even move. Instead, he smiled.

"You have given me a speech," Paweł said, and then Gracian. "You have chosen to do this. But I have told you that I will work for you and work hard, to keep myself living. And it seems to me that what is needed is not words but work. You see, I have been told other words too, Herr Foreman. Other speeches. About the importance to you of the coal in this country of ours. About the shortage of good men and the need for more production. These things you need, but you do not speak of needs but only of countries and of philosophies. That is a shame for every man in this room."

He stood. He rebuttoned his woollen jacket.

"But now, as you are saying, I must go."

And then there was a sigh and the crackle of paper, and the newspaper man folded his broadsheet and placed it down before him. For the first time he looked up at Paweł. By the wall, Albert Schwabe was looking at the back of his hand, his cigarette spent. When the newspaper man spoke, it was in Polish but with a heavy German inflection.

"Mr. Sófka," he said, "my name is Karl Gintse. *I* am the foreman of this colliery. I will give you work. You will work shift B, which starts at five-thirty tomorrow morning. Report here at five for your details. A partner will be assigned to train you. You may leave."

Paweł paused and then nodded. He looked at Gracian, placed a calming hand on his shoulder blade, and ushered him out of the room.

Because the wind had subsided and because the snow brushed their ankles with pale blue shadow, the journey home passed quickly. Yet the cold had honed the air to slate and the slate slid through the brothers' clothes to their skin. There was no respite.

As they walked, Gracian's mind was full of questions. Paweł had given him no reaction to the events at the colliery, and his silence hung between them. Gracian had no idea where or by what means to broach it.

It was Paweł who spoke first. He was some strides ahead, and for an instant Gracian could not be sure the voice he heard was his brother's.

"You mustn't think about what was said in that room," the voice said. He slowed to let Gracian draw up beside him. "You must learn things yourself and not through the mouths of others. You must think about them in your own time. Whatever you heard was my concern, and my concern only, understand, brother?"

"I understand," he said.

They walked together, the sound of snow creaking compacted under boot soles; beneath that the rattle of breeze through bare branches.

Then Gracian saw Paweł's wide shoulders sag and his pace slow until he had stopped. He saw Paweł lift his head up and take a deep sigh inward, swelling his chest as if for the first breath. Gracian too had stopped, and now he waited.

"I'm sorry," Paweł said.

Gracian thought of the hum of electric insects and the smell of smoke and the rustle of paper. "I told you I'd come," he said.

"What? Oh. No, brother, I meant for speaking to you like that. Like Mother would."

Paweł turned suddenly and looked at Gracian. His face was veined and flushed as if after physical effort.

"The trouble with families," he said slowly, with care, "is that sometimes they try to bind themselves so tight they become blind with the effort of it, and then the blindness infects them and threatens everything they once were or might be. I do not know if a family in this blind state can ever find a cure. I think blindness is usually permanent."

He turned his face away from Gracian's now and looked again out into the winter nothing.

"And the trouble with decisions," he continued, "is that no matter how hard you try to keep them separate, to make space for them and then go on as before, they will always break free. And then nothing is as it was. Like water in a leaking bucket—a tiny leak you thought impossible, that you thought you'd patched—old decisions will find ways to trickle out and ruin everything. No matter how hard I've tried, it always happens."

Gracian waited for him to speak further but he did not.

"I think I understand," he said. He was shivering from the cold. But Paweł did not seem to feel it.

"And I'm sorry," Paweł said. "I'm sorry for those."

He lifted his arm and pointed to the space above their heads. Gracian looked up and saw the sky had dusked. Here and there a few white daylight clouds remained. In the upper night could be seen the dim shine of stars growing brighter.

"I know you miss them."

Gracian wanted badly to look up but could think of nothing now but the cold. He had begun to shift from foot to foot to keep the shivers down. His teeth were chattering.

Paweł looked at his younger brother slap-hugging himself and shuffling, and then looked at the swirl of snow upon the ground, and Gracian thought he heard him laugh. Then Paweł kicked up a spray of white and began to walk again.

They were among the first streets of Maleńkowice and then they were further in and then they were close to the Malewskas' flat. Paweł said he would be leaving him here, and as he said it he glanced at Gracian. He halted and stopped Gracian with his hands and looked at him with urgency.

"Gracian! Your hat is undone!" Paweł said.

It was true. Along the walk the boy had been lost to his thoughts and his hat straps had slipped his mind. Instinctively he raised his hand to his right ear, and Paweł slapped it quickly away.

But not quick enough. Not quick enough to stop him from feeling that the lobe of his ear had become hard and brittle and to feel a bright razor pain through his cheekbone.

"How long has it been undone?" Paweł said.

"What's wrong with it?" Gracian said breathlessly.

"How *long*?"

"From the beginning, maybe." He could feel it now, the burning of it. "What is it?"

"Frostbite! Frostbite, you idiot boy! Cover it, we have to get to the house."

"I can go myself."

"Quiet, Gracian, walk faster."

They approached the house from the back, passing the old crab-apple tree. In panic Gracian ran to the door, but Paweł had the scruff of his collar and dragged him back.

"Stay. We have to warm it slowly."

He bent down and took his glove off and tucked it into his pocket and then with his three-fingered hand scooped up snow and held it between his thumb and fingers as one would hold something precious. He told Gracian to lift the flap of his hat, and he examined the ear and then rubbed the snow gently into it.

He told Gracian to wait, and for a time they waited. Then Paweł opened the door and walked in, pulled a chair close to the door, and told Gracian to sit on it.

"Sit here. In fifteen minutes close the door."

"What will happen?"

"It will heal. I think we've saved it."

Paweł turned to leave and Gracian watched him.

"Paweł," he heard himself say. His voice was so quiet he thought Paweł would not hear it. But Paweł stopped and paused where he stood.

"I know what you said about forgetting. But that man said you were in prison."

Gracian saw a bright silver gun nestled in cloth the colour of midnight.

Paweł tapped his hand against his thigh and sniffed in the cold.

"A long time ago, Gracian," he said. "That leak has been fixed," he said.

Then he left.

When Gracian's mother discovered him alone on the chair with frostbite in his ear she shouted at him until her throat was sore. When he told her that Paweł had a job at colliery Osok, she stopped and stared at him, and her lips were open a little.

"Well, that's something," she said eventually, covering the hole of her mouth with one hand.

During the evening Gracian's ear swelled. It swelled and it would not stop swelling. By nightfall his earlobe had become the size of a heavy fruit, like a springtime orange. The growth was pink and translucent and gave a shock of pain when touched. It brought an itching deep down in the base of his skull. When Gracian ran his fingers gingerly across its surface he felt the strangeness of his own body expanded beyond its natural horizons. He looked at it in the small square of mirror among the shadows of his room and examined the intricate patina on its thin-stretched globe, felt its stupid bobbing weight as he moved his head. He turned this way and that and glimpsed the presence of its curvatures in the corners of his eyes.

This is what it's like, he thought to himself. *This is what it's like to be changed beyond all expectation.*

In the morning Gracian's mother heated a darning needle over a pan of boiling water and handed it to him. As she turned away he saw that the skin about her eyes was swollen.

He pricked it himself. When it burst it released a measure of clear liquid, a miniature river flowing from his head.

Later, at the mine, the men elbowed him and teased him about his bandaged ear.

"That's what happens when you listen to Gerard Dylong for too long," they said.

Some days later Gracian found Paweł waiting for him once more by the gates. Around one eye there was a fading bruise, yet he seemed relaxed.

"You've had a fight," Gracian said.

"Perhaps. How is your ear?"

A thick pale crust had formed upon the earlobe and it itched ceaselessly.

"Fine."

"And how are Mother and Sister?"

"Mother's been crying."

Paweł was silent.

"Will you come with me? For a short time?" he said then.

They walked to the Malewskas' flat. Neither Anna nor her family were to be seen. Paweł told him to wait where he was and left the room. One of Anna's dresses was draped over a chair back, and below that lay a pair of her shoes. In the empty room, Gracian wanted to go over and touch them.

Paweł returned some time later with a large battered cardboard box in his arms.

"Here," Paweł said, giving Gracian the box.

"Why?" said Gracian.

"No questions. There is one thing, before you look. You must never show this or mention it to any person. Only you and I must know of it. Understand?"

"I understand."

"Do you swear, brother?"

"I swear."

Gracian opened the box. Inside was bedding made of crumpled strips of paper and on top of the paper was the most wonderful thing Gracian had ever seen. He looked at it for a long time and then, as careful as if he had a baby in his hands, he lifted it out.

There it was.

A telescope.

Two

The telescope consisted of three cylinders of brass-hued metal, each with a thin gun-silver rim encircling the ends. Four rims in all. The thinnest cylinder, as thick as a small tree branch or a hand-axe handle, could slide into the second cylinder, which again could slide into the last. Then the whole thing was no longer and no more wide than a wine bottle. The sliding took some effort; the action was halting and stubborn, as if the telescope found no dignity in its own reduction. There were dents in the metal of the cylinders, signs of wear and usage. But the lenses were clear and true and without blemish. Weighed on upturned palms the telescope was surprisingly light, as if it might splinter like parchment if dropped, its secret lost forever.

Gracian knew from experience that certain objects seem to possess a soul, or at least hold within them a store of memories and experiences that can be read upon their surfaces like type. He felt this of the telescope from the moment he saw it on its paper bed. He felt the life of it and heard its calls to him, a music of glass and metal. Images came to him all at once.

He imagined the telescope in the hands of a sailor on some storm-stung sea. He saw its skin reflecting the lightning, prying a space between black-heaped clouds, rain spattering the metal with the sound of frying oil.

He saw it in the hands of an assassin. There in some distant country crouched among the baking rocks above an encampment, moving slowly from one far-off figure to the next, registering faces, gestures, habits, uncovering and remembering, pointing down like an arrow from its owner's eye; as if the telescope brought the first death, the real death, before the bullet.

Last, he placed it in the hands of a blind man, brought up and pressed against the fragile bulb of his eye. The blind man stood on a balcony that hung over an ancient town draped in blue light. He stood there casting a long shadow on the balcony floor with the telescope raised to his veiled eye.

For the blind man, Gracian saw, this was a great and unfading pleasure, an imaginary magnification of a world he had known only in his imagination, a sweet reassurance that the vistas he saw in his mind were as real in detail as any other. For when the blind man looked through the telescope, the lens projected only what the viewer already kept within him.

But Gracian did not lift it to his own eye until later that night, when he had reached home and stood in his room with the doors closed and no lamp lit. Earlier he had gone downstairs to the brick-tower heater that stood in the corner of Francesca's room. He had dragged over the hessian sack of coal, which belched out black puffs and stained his hands, and he had opened the iron grille at the base of the tower and shovelled in coal, stoked it, and closed the grille. Then he had gone into the kitchen to eat with his family, the telescope concealed in the deep inner pocket of his coat, which hung on his chair. The suspense of it was nearly impossible to bear.

In a few hours the sky was completely dark and the brick tower had radiated its heat to the upper reaches of the house. Gracian got up from the table, hiding his eagerness to climb the stairs, and the curious eyes of his mother and his sister watched him disappear from them, his coat bundled in his arms and the telescope inside like the heart of a sleeping animal.

Only the top pane of the small window in his room could be opened, and Gracian hauled it down. Then to give himself height he dragged over the old dusty clothes trunk. It had belonged in turn to his grandfather, whom Gracian had never known, and his father. His father had used it when he was in the army during the Great War. On one side it said sófka in peeling gold letters. He stood up on it before the window and felt the chill air on his face and the clinging warmth of the room on his back and neck, as if he were rising up half submerged from a gentle sea. His ear was nearly healed and no longer throbbed in the cold.

Then slowly, ceremoniously, he looked through the eyepiece of the telescope.

The difference was this: Lying back in the viewing place with his father's magnifying glass before him, the stars had revealed themselves to him in two layers, one within the other. The first was the flat wide ground of the sky; flat, yet of that depth of darkness in which the eye loses itself. The second was in the round frame of the glass, the stars there gorged and indistinct, the sky slightly grainy as if drained of substance. In this way, he had transformed the star-strung sky into a page for his perusal, examining the stars together in their scattering and then subjecting a portion to closer scrutiny. And each layer was distinct; Gracian could move his eye from one to the other at will.

But the telescope sucked Gracian up through it into a singular universe, a looming, shivering place whose vibrations were numerous and often wild, responsive to the beat of his heart and the hot blood-swell through his hands. Here the stars were no longer a multitude and instead became a few fat round shimmers, light blurs of great brightness and beauty and seemingly so near that the boy reached out a hand out to feel them and was surprised to find his fingers groping through nothing.

There were no longer layers but a concave concentration, a oneness. Everything about looking through the telescope, it seemed to Gracian, was singular. One eye squeezed shut, hiking up the corner of his mouth, the other wide open against the single hole. The entirety of vision was channelled through that hole, that open eye, pulling him whole into the giant stars so far away. An upward flow. Circles within circles.

For the first time, Gracian was able to see things the book with faded red letters on cream had spoken of. He could make out the faint forms of stars that had evaded him. He could see the hazy colourations that meant he was looking perhaps at another planet or perhaps another moon. And though he could no longer see the constellations complete, he could trace out their patterns, as if in doing so he were giving them life.

Through the metal eye, Gracian's world was restored to him. Each day he waited patiently to greet it again. For a time everything inside him felt well and at peace, and he thought what he felt was a kind of love. He had a new secret now, and to look through the telescope was to surrender to its power.

Christmas came and went. Gracian's mother could secure only a single carp from the salesman who came each year from the breeding rivers in the south. She had to bribe him twenty deutsche marks. No one made an effort to invite Paweł; in any case, there was too little food for his inviting. But his absence had hung in the room like a void, a ripple of the air. Gracian ate with his mother and Francesca and Józef Kukła and the baby. There was little talk.

"This is *good,* Mother," Francesca had said, speaking through a forkload of carp. "There really is plenty."

"Yes!" said Kukła; then, turning to Gracian, "Your mother could make a broth with hot water and a rusty nail!" It was an old joke. His father used to make it. Kukła laughed too loudly, slapping his knee.

Gracian looked at the stars. The viewing place, like the imprint of a breath against a windowpane, was fast fading from his memory. He began to talk and joke again with Gerard Dylong and the other men at the mine and felt an easiness return to his steps as he walked through the village, though the easiness had a limit and the limit affected all the villagers. The attacks by the local special police, whom the villagers called by the German term *Schupo,* had worsened. There were four or five of them, youths from the surrounding region, in age not far off from Gracian, who would patrol the village threatening those who passed. Gracian had heard of at least three beatings and had himself met their stares on his way back from the colliery. Józef Kukła had begun to come home later from work in the bakery, to avoid their patrol. Even Old Man Morek cut his songs short. And Gerard Dylong said he had been spat at.

"They spat in my face yesterday in the street," he said. "They were so young their uniforms hardly fit them. Those green hats falling off their heads. I could have killed them all. I thought that, to myself, y'understand? I could have snapped their necks like twigs and left them broken." He shrugged his heavy shoulders. "But what then, Galileo? Then this world might well have lost the best coal miner it's got. It would be like robbing the world." He leaned over and patted the coal face. "And I would never have found my treasure." His smile was like its own lamp in the dimness.

Through the telescope Gracian learned to see again.

Though at first it was the stars alone that occupied his sight, over time a change occurred. After he had had his fill of the constellations, Gracian's muscles would lengthen after the work of the day and he would often fall into a weariness. At these times he would transfer his gaze to matters closer: to the fixtures of his room, to the empty cracked concrete of the yard with its vegetable patches strangled bare by the winter. He came to enjoy this shift of perspective and spent some time indulging in it, for he found the pleasure of looking at the sky made keener by the pleasure of looking at the world around him.

There were times, too, after work, when the afternoon balanced on the edge of evening, that Gracian found himself alone in the house. He had begun to stand in Francesca and Kukła's room, where the window gave a clear view of the curve of the main street. The texture of the cobblestones, the dim traces of figures behind darkened windows, the expressions on the faces of those who passed, all were laid out before him. He stood entranced, his coat close at hand so he might conceal the telescope if anyone came back to the house unexpectedly.

It was on one of these occasions, viewing the street outside, that out of the corner of his eye Gracian noticed a spider. It was crawling down the white flaking window frame, its feet barely alighting on the wood. Distracted, the boy glanced at it and saw it slip on the bevel of a frame divider and tumble suddenly into empty space above the pane. And just as he thought the insect had lost its fight with gravity, it stopped falling and hung there suspended, legs dangling limp like the hand of a dying man.

Without thinking he turned the telescope upon it,

finding that he had to step back some paces to let the creature come into focus in the lens. Now the spider was a mass of bristling hairs protruding from the round nub of body and the junctured skeletal legs. In a moment, though, the spider recovered itself and began to climb up its invisible thread, and Gracian could see its workings like those of a machine with its casing off: the synchronized flexures of the limbs, a set of tiny pistons; the pincers clutching, strong, enduring.

It seemed to Gracian at that moment that there existed in the world two visions, each at an extreme. One saw the world from a great height or distance and the other from hardly any distance at all. Both visions were full of intricate sights, a whole universe of them, but normally these lay beyond the reach of man. The vision held and lived by men was a pale, weak thing compared to the other two visions, which, Gracian thought, might be called the true visions. The vision of man existed at neither one extreme nor the other but in an unrevealing haze between the two: an unlit, compromised vision, offering nothing beautiful to the eye.

It was possible for man to gain passing access to the true visions, as he himself had done. Through the surrogate eye of a telescope this could be achieved, or through other means equally unsatisfying—a book of history, perhaps, that spoke of the great roll of ages, or the reflection in a morning dewdrop, or perhaps the view of the land on a clear day atop an empty tor. But for man to achieve one of the true visions, he must always forsake the other. Both universes at once, the far and the near, were beyond his grasp. See the grace of a spider's movement and miss the structure of its body; see the structure, and miss the movement. One or the other. Such were the choices.

If only, Gracian thought, there was a way of reconciling the two. To see truly and with both eyes together. Then what secret might be unveiled? What story might at last be told?

But even in the urgent beating of his mind and of his heart, there beside the cool transparency of the window and the scrabbling of the spider, he knew this to be impossible. It was the fate of man to see with eyes unlike the stars'. Eyes weighted to earth, their scope always stopping short of forever.

On an evening soon after he had seen the spider, Gracian sat in his empty room thinking about Paweł. He had not seen his brother since he had given him the telescope, though he still half expected to meet him one afternoon leaning against the colliery gates amid the snow. He did not know if Paweł was holding his job in Osok, but he supposed from his lack of contact with the family that he was. His mother did not ask after him, though he knew her thoughts wandered frequently to her elder son, for when they did she would draw herself up, flexing her jaw as if to brace herself. One day Gracian had thought about visiting him, but had turned back embarrassed less than halfway to the Malewskas' flat. If Paweł wanted to see him, he told himself, he would make himself seen. Until then, their lives were best left to trace their separate tracks.

The evening was drawing close around him, and he sat on his bed with his boots off feeling the hardness of the mattress beneath him and listening to the wind blow the snow outside. The telescope lay some distance away from him, on the cabinet that stood beside Paweł's bed. The round blank lens was facing at an angle toward him, and he saw his own face reflected, stretched upward and ghostly in the circular darkness. For a moment he did not recognize it; the chin was too defined, the cheeks too narrow, the eyes had about them an intensity. The image he saw was of a man and not a boy.

He stood quickly, dug his hands into his trouser pockets, and scraped his fingertips against the rough inner cloth. Then he walked out of the room and paused in the hallway. He could hear his mother and Francesca talking, their voices coming to him as if through water. He turned and walked to the room in which his mother slept and placed his hand upon the doorknob. He turned it slowly, wincing with expectation of the noise that would alert them, but none came, and he swung the door open and walked inside. It smelled of his mother there, fragrant and with an under-spice that reminded him of being a small child close to her. He moved to the chest of drawers that stood at the foot of the bed in the small unaired room and opened the bottom of the five drawers. This was his father's drawer, where his mother kept mementos: a bundle of yellowed letters tied with string; a seashell shaped like an ear; reading glasses, coated now with dust; a pair of rolling dice; a watch that no longer ran, and whose snapped strap his father had worn mended with sealing tape. And photographs.

He picked up the slim pile of pictures and shuffled through them until he found what he had been looking for. It was a photograph with white lacy paper edges taken by one of his father's friends with a new box camera some years after the war, the black now ebbed to brown and the white to cream. His father looked young; he was standing in his work clothes in the soft shadows of a summer morning glade in the forest, a smile just breaking across his wide face. For some years he had done a seasonal job felling trees, and here he stood with one boot up on a tree stump looking like some popular hero or explorer, the long axe over his shoulder. Behind him other men were working. He couldn't have been more than twenty-eight or twenty-nine years old.

Gracian had not set his eyes on this photograph for some time, and the youth and strength of the man he saw there seemed strange to him. He turned the picture about briefly in the filtered half-light, letting the moon sheen the surface, and then pushed it into his shirt pocket and hurried out.

In the quiet of his room he took it out and placed it on the window ledge to let the light from outside illuminate it. He did not wish to light the lamps, for in the encroaching darkness he felt a sanctity and the sanctity seemed fitting. He manoeuvered the picture so that it lay vertically on the ledge before him, his father's face facing his. Then he stepped away and back, moved again over to the photograph, closed one eye, and lifted the telescope.

In such close-up the features of his father's face shimmered and dispersed into granules. Gracian did not know what he was looking for among them; perhaps for the shadow of the disease that later ravaged him, perhaps for the fainter shadows of his own face. Yet as he looked, other pictures with sharper focus began to crowd the lens, moving, bringing their brightness upward to him.

His father sitting at the end of his bed in a room choked with light and heat despite the open window. Tomorrow was Gracian's ninth birthday.

What would you like, boy? his father was saying in that way he spoke: Silesian dialect, more old Slav than Polish. What would you most like to have?

Gracian propped himself up on his elbows. A finch, he said, imagining the bird in his palm. A golden finch.

His father frowned. And how do you expect to get one of those?

I don't know. But I've wanted one all my life.

There were creases in the corners of his father's eyes. All your life? You haven't lived yet. You have a whole past to earn.

How?

You earn it by years lived.

But I do want one. I have a cage for it. I made it myself. From wood.

That's no cage, boy. That's a box. A finch needs to feel free.

It will. It will feel free. I'll make sure.

His father's big rough hand patting his head, messing his hair, fingers stained the colour of amber from all the rolling tobacco he smoked. Well. We'll see.

The next day his father had gone to work in the forest.

The story was that in the midday heat he had seen a nest of finches high up in a birch, squawking as their mother fed them. He laid down his equipment and tested the grip of the bark and then began to climb the tree. He climbed until he reached the nest. While he was trying to cup one of the young birds in his hand the mother bird had dived down from the higher branches, eyes like angry pearls, beating her wings to keep steady and biting at his fingers. He dropped the young bird and grabbed at the trunk, but he knew he had lost it and fell in a hurtling daze of green and yellow. He hit the ground and lay there panting, shocked. Some of the men gathered around him and offered him their hands to pull him off the ground. But he had just brushed them away and got to his feet and shook his head, as if to clear it of a thought, and then made his way back up the tree.

He came home that night with scratches all over him. He strode over to his son and scooped him up against him so the boy could smell him, smoke and sweat.

How's my boy? he said, and then put him down. I have something for you.

Where? Where? What is it?

He turned to his side and nodded down at his jacket pocket. Have a look.

Gracian, breathing heavy with expectation, hooked one finger over the rim of his father's pocket, pulled it open a little and peered in.

The baby finch sat among a small soft cloud of mustard feathers. Its crown was a little black thumb pressing down onto vivid red, its head was darting to its own bird rhythms, its eye was an opal, and from its tiny beak came soft chirpings. Gracian let it hop onto his hand and took it out for all to see.

It'll feel free, he said.

Later his father made him a proper cage from a wooden disc and strands of silver wire. He kept that bird in his room for two years. The day after his father died, it escaped through the wire and soared out into the yard.

It was deepest night now, when the sun is most distant from the earth. Gracian took the photograph from the sill and dropped it on the bed, letting it slip from his hand as a man might let slip a used wrapper or spent ticket. He stood by the window and saw the yard and the forest beyond that.

Something pulled his eye into focus, a warp of movement out among the shadows of the field beyond the yard. A small black shape was passing from each tree shadow to the next, as if made from the same substance as the darkness. It was making its way slowly, moving in bursts, quick and agile, leaping, stopping, vanishing, and then returning, in a wide zigzag motion down the face of the field. Gracian felt the small hairs rise up on his scalp. He thought what he saw was a phantom, born from the wanderings of his thoughts. But the closer it came, rushing out across the dark earth, the surer Gracian became of its reality.

Finally he remembered the telescope in his hand. He slid the chest over with the outside of his foot and stepped up onto it and tried to force the top pane further down to give him better vantage. It gave only a few inches before he felt it wedge there. He raised the telescope.

It was gone. There was nothing but the fields and the still air, in which seemed to hang low motes of dust, catching moonlight. As he moved the telescope in a small parabola around his eye, the scene became nervous, halting to right itself and then shattering again.

And then, finally, movement renewed. The spirit had detached itself from the far edge of the field and was passing quickly over an area of white. The boy could see that it left behind it a trail of shallow pockmarks in relief against the snow.

Footprints. It was, then, a figure. A man. A man running.

The man had reached the low end of the field and was almost at the perimeter wall of the backyard, and when he reached it he stopped. He bent down to catch his breath, his open mouth visible, and then stood again. Although Gracian could see the man now, see the muted colours and contours of his body and even a little detail on his hat and coat, both of which were as black as the trousers and shoes, he could not quite make out the face. It would not remain stationary and there was too much shadow; the hat drawn low over the brow seemed to leak its darkness onto the skin below.

Instead of moving on, the man seemed to be waiting. He had crooked one hand up onto his side as if to depress a stitch and the other hand was stroking his chin and so further obscuring his face to Gracian. The man was gazing out into the field beyond the rectangle of space prescribed by the window frame, and Gracian knew he had no chance of looking where the man looked.

Some emotion was transforming the figure. His body became more animated, his arms coming down to his sides and hanging tensed, and then he bent himself over a little, his head facing side on to Gracian at the window. He was gesturing beyond Gracian's frame of vision, sweeping his hand toward himself, mouthing urgent but inaudible words.

Then came another figure, also dressed in black, running in from the left. The boy's grip on the telescope tightened. The figure came running, and the man opened his arms and embraced it, lifting it a foot or more from the ground. By the size and movement of this second figure, Gracian could tell it was a woman.

The man and the woman stood together in the cold silence. Then the man glanced around and gestured toward the wall, and with sudden grace both of them had vaulted it and were in the yard.

They were in the yard! The boy withdrew swiftly from the window, aware for the first time that he might be seen. He reasoned with himsef: They were still a distance away and without the aid of a telescope. They could not see him. He swallowed air and reapproached the window.

They were sitting with their backs against the wall and

the man was leaning forward, talking to the woman. She appeared not to be looking at him but concentrating on her breathing, her chin lowered and her arms resting on her outstretched legs, bent at the elbows and palms upward like a doll's. But now she was reaching up and laying her hand on the man's face, the heel of it against his ear. And this action of hers must have been a sign, for the man stopped talking. He stopped talking and they looked at each other for a long time. Then slowly their two heads came together in a kiss.

Gracian thought their lips would part but they didn't and instead the kiss became something different; it became a joining. Their heads in the darkness became the movement of one thing. And now the man was leaning forward and inward, not sitting anymore but almost kneeling, pressing into the woman. His hand and then his arm was against her stomach, and the woman, too, pressed into the man, pressing back with her own weight, their hands moving over each other slowly, then faster. Slowly, then faster, with the man's head now buried in the crook of the woman's neck and his hands disappearing into the darkness of them both, and though the moonlight struck stark the shifting surfaces of them, still the faces were unknowable. They went down slowly together now on the lucent ground, easing down; he could see the taut folds on the man's sleeves. Then the man was lifting the woman's torso from underneath, so that her head tipped back loose and came up to meet the man's in a kiss renewed and there was a rhythm to it. There was a rhythm to it, how the man reached down, dragging his hands over her black skirt folds, which Gracian only now could see. Dragging his hands back and upward, lifting the black fabric of the skirt, the whites of her thighs showing in the night. And then he was over them, between them, and the both of them moving, moving together, their breaths bright coils of white.

And their breaths were Gracian's breaths, loud in his ears, and their fingers were his fingers keeping the lens steady.

And their movement filled him with something he had felt before without placing it, and their movement coated them both with snow, so that the ground below them was a dark bare ring, and the stars shone wide above them, and then they were slowing and slowing and slowing until they were no longer moving, frozen.

He had been balancing on the chest and now his socked feet slipped, the telescope hitting the window frame. He could feel the nerves below his skin and in his muscles and could barely lift it back to his eye.

When he did he saw both figures moving swiftly back out along the exterior wall and slipping past its perimeter and around the outer edge of the house. Gracian ran out of the room. He went down the stairs two and three at a time and now he did not care who he woke, for a hot desire had bloomed within him and he jumped the last steps onto the floor and half skidded, half padded, taking long strides into the kitchen and to the window. There was no noise in the house. He pressed his hands and face against the cold glass and stared into the void beyond the side wall, knowing he was too late. He turned his face and crushed his cheek flat against the glass. Far away down the street two shapes like flapping black rags were vanishing along the house edges.

And still he had not seen their faces. But he had seen

enough. Enough of the sleepy, loping gait—so like his own—and the wide back of the one, and enough of the hair darker than night and the long arms of the other. He had seen enough. He knew Paweł Sófka and he knew Anna Malewska; he knew them well.

It was a new year. January 1941. The snows fell less often. Far away in Africa, the British and the Australians and the Germans were fighting a war for Tobruk.

The next night Gracian waited for them to come, but they did not come. The night after that he waited for them to come, but still they did not come.

Two nights after that the man was there at three in the morning, racing down across the field. This time when he reached the wall of the yard he paused, and Gracian got his first conclusive look. It was Paweł all right, out of breath and breathing hard. But Anna did not join him that night, and in moments he had gone.

Over the space of the next fortnight Gracian watched every night, often sleeping for some hours in the late afternoon to keep strength for the night. Five times he saw his brother emerging from the distant forest, each time taking the same route down to and around the yard. Five times too he saw his brother moving in the opposite direction, slipping out from the darkness to appear before the wall and then making his way by the same method up toward the forest. He would appear from the same place between the trees, sometimes an hour later, sometimes two, sometimes more, and come back down.

Once or twice Gracian thought he saw more figures flitting by the hem of the forest, but he couldn't be sure. Sometimes Paweł seemed as before to be waiting for someone or for a sign that Gracian could not see. But if it was Anna he was waiting for, she didn't come to him.

At first he had wondered: Did they come here every night? Had he been missing this silent congress so close below the window? Was this a habit of theirs, to meet and kiss and lie upon each other on the cold floor of the yard? But why would they do such a thing? Out of necessity? Because it pleased them?

At first he had wondered: Did Paweł want him to see these things?

But as he watched his brother come and go without Anna more and more often, he began to see it was another meeting he had been missing. Some other meeting bigger than the one that had made him wait through the hours with the telescope clutched in his fingers, wait despite his desperate weariness, because his nerves were taut in expectation and desire.

Along the yard edge, across the field, inside the forest, something else was happening.

Gracian had felt a curiosity about Paweł since he could

remember anything he thought important about himself. Like all else, he had learned to get used to it. But this new discovery, of which Paweł could not be aware, had lifted a tiny lid inside him, and he felt it lift, and now he was sick of not knowing. He wanted to know, to know *something*.

Because Paweł might find himself in danger. Because there were lives for the living outside of his own. Because of what he had seen in the stark moonlight, where two bodies could find themselves entangled so tightly that there seemed no hope of their parting.

✦

He asked his sister first, going to her room after work. He had washed himself quickly in the shower rooms, and the black dust was still on his hands and in the creases of his neck and in slivers beneath his fingernails.

He knocked on the door and pushed it open and stood sheepish in the frame. Francesca sat on her bed with the baby at her breast, her finger delicately holding open the rough crease of her blouse. She looked up at the noise of him, her eyes preoccupied. Her face was distracted, shiny.

"Gracian. What is it?"

He had been preparing for this all day, but now the force went out of him. He simply stood in the doorway with his hands in his pockets, stirring the floor dust with a boot tip.

"What's the matter? Can't you see I'm busy?"

The baby had stopped his suckling and was making movements with his mouth, opening, closing. His little hands searched the air and his wide eyes roamed. Francesca pressed him back into place against her.

"Francesca . . . I . . . I've been thinking."

"About what?"

"Nothing. It's nothing."

The baby starting to make noises like water in a pipe.

"Then why are you still here? What's bothering you?"

"I've been thinking about Paweł."

"Oh, yes? Well, he's certainly done a lot to think about recently."

"He has? Like what? What has he been doing?"

"Don't be stupid. Refusing to work, first. Fighting with Józef like that. Storming out. Never calling on us. I don't care if he has a job now, he needs to apologize. There needs to be respect. You understand, Gracian, there has to be respect between families, especially now."

"Yes. But . . ." Gracian ran his dirty hand across his hair, smearing his forehead. "But I was thinking about it before. About Paweł before. When I was little. I know he did some things. No one ever told me what. I—"

Francesca sighed loudly then. The baby, startled, started gurgling.

"Oh," she said flatly, as if making an announcement. She lowered the baby onto her lap and began to rock it slowly on her knee. Up, down, up, down. The baby made a sound like *sha!* and fell silent.

Francesca was looking out with steady brown eyes under glossy lids. Looking at her little brother.

"Listen to me, Gracian," she said. "I have enough wars

to fight. My own battles. I don't have time for this one, and I have even less time for those of the past. Ask someone else. Or, on second thought, don't. Don't ask anyone. Just don't ask at all."

She had said all she would. Quietly she set the groggy child on her lap and began rebuttoning her blouse.

Gracian nodded, took hold of the doorknob, and began to close the door. When there was only the smallest slit of light visible between the door and its frame he heard Francesca's voice again.

"Gracian," she said, "just forget it. You'll know someday. You just picked a bad time, that's all. Bad time for all of us."

Two days later he got a chance to raise the subject with Kukła. He felt somehow that this gaunt, guarded man might be willing to speak. And again he was wrong. They sat together alone in the kitchen in the fading dusk. It had been a day of exceptional brightness, the snow-covering a mirror for a high white sun. Only evening had brought relief.

Kukła was filling his pipe and reading one of his novels, *Latarnik*. It was his favourite. He had read it six or seven times while Gracian had known him. When he sat down Kukła glanced up from it, said, "Hello, boy," and lapsed back into silence.

After a time Gracian said, "It's still cold."

Kukła did not look up or break his reading. "Will be for a time."

"Must be warm in the bakery."

"Too warm. Like hell, boy."

Gracian sniffed and leaned in his chair, making it creak. "Wonder what Paweł is doing?" He tried to say this vaguely, as if it were a question that had merely leaked from his lips and was directed to the air.

"Don't say that name near me," Kukła said with no change in his tone.

It was very quiet. Perhaps the snow was falling again, for the falling of the snow seemed to smother sound. The beams of the house groaned somewhere.

"Just thinking," the boy said.

Slowly Kukła placed the book open and face down on the table.

"Your brother is a kind of animal. Don't ever think otherwise. He thinks he has charm, he thinks he's full of puzzles like a circus magician with flowers up his sleeves. But there's nothing there. Nothing but his own dirty animal selfishness. Don't forget it, boy. And don't go upsetting your mother and the rest of this house by bringing him up here."

He pushed his chair back and stood and picked up his pipe and walked out of the room.

Gracian sat still, staring at the book lying spine upward in front of him and at the reflection of the book in the polished wood. After a minute Kukła came back, retrieved the book, tucked it under his arm, and left again.

He didn't ask his mother. He couldn't expect anything from her.

Gracian thought of Gerard Dylong only later, on his shift, after they'd blown the first charges of the morning. In recent times Dylong's efforts to find the store of sulphur had seemed to intensify. Now instead of running his palms across the coal face he would lay the whole of himself against it and reach his hands up on either side in a slow circle. His big hands would skit and flutter against the rock and his eyelids too would flutter in his head and his pink tongue tip would come out from between his lips. To see this giant of a man pressing himself there was both comic and peculiar, and Gracian would often lower his eyes or turn away to tend the explosives when Dylong was prospecting like this.

Dylong's efforts were never all in vain. They were clearing record amounts of coal with each blast because of Dylong's instructions where to bore. And because each clearing revealed no sulphur, Dylong worked them both hard and strong to clear the coal to blast again, and Gracian's weariness from staying awake far into each night could not reach him, because Dylong gave him a power in his blood that sprang straight from that man's driven soul.

"Drill *there,* not *there,*" Dylong was saying now, pointing to his markings. "Don't get it wrong, Galileo, don't ever get it wrong."

Watching Dylong there against the coal face, the idea came to Gracian almost with the force of a revelation. He remembered how he had once asked the veteran where he had learned his skills. At this, Dylong had laid down his hand axe and folded his arms. "The coal is a mystery to be unravelled," he had said. "First you must teach yourself the nature of the mystery. Then you can start looking for the solution."

He waited until they sat, as was their habit, side by side against the slatted wall braces, passing between them a single unfiltered cigarette burning in the carbide glow. In the quiet, Gracian wondered to himself about the solution Dylong had spoken of. He wondered at what moment Dylong had concluded that the riddle of coal had only a single possible answer: sulphur, green and pure.

What a curse it was, Gracian thought, to know the answer, yet never to find it.

He took a deep inhalation, rested the ball of his skull against the wall brace, and felt the smoke fill his body with its musty breath. He closed his eyes, saw the redness of his eyelids, and passed the cigarette back over to Dylong. His arms ached, deep in the tendons.

"Well, well, well," Dylong was muttering, shaking his head as if in disbelief or perhaps mournfulness, whispering to himself. "Next time, next time." He took the cigarette and put it to his lips and sucked on it and exhaled through mouth and nose. He tried to spit out a few stray strands of tobacco that clung to his lip, making a noise like *thpt-thpt,* but failed and had to pick them away with indelicate fingers.

"Dylong?" Gracian said, rolling his head over in Dylong's direction.

"What is it, Galileo?"

"In your life. You've seen a lot of things?"

Dylong gave a laugh that turned into a cough. He bent forward, pressing his thick chest against his knees. He looked at Gracian and then looked back again. He scooped up a piece of rubble from the flooring before him, moved it about in his palm. Then he launched into speech.

"I have been a miner for forty years. I started when I was twelve. Saw two collapses in my career. Twenty-five men dead in the worst one, ten of them trapped for six hours, choked in the coal dust. I saw the people of this place rise up and find themselves, two long months in the spring of 1921. It took more than a vote—took blood, boy, took too much blood, going back years. Saw my own father wounded in the chest by the *Freikorps,* early 1919. He hardly spoke after that.

"Had women, many young women. Beautiful women. Had a wife the best of them all. Had a son. Not for long, but I had one, a beautiful son. I saw the Germans come in convoys over the hills, starved and pale like old women.

Saw them fill their mouths up with Polish sausage, bread, butter, till they were shitting themselves in the fields. Shitting themselves and vomiting, right there in the grass, I'm telling you."

He nodded at the empty space before them.

"You could say I've seen things, Galileo. You could say my eyes are all full up with seeing."

Gracian considered the words. "Do you ever think of it all?" he said. "The past?" he said.

"The past should be left to the past," Dylong said.

"I've been thinking about it," Gracian said.

Dylong glanced at him. Old ruddy skin, ingrained with coal. A smile trace lifting a cheekbone. "Ha," he said.

"I've lived," the boy said. "And things have happened. People have done things. I know they've done things, and I want to know about them. It's time that I knew, Dylong."

"What are you so worked up about?" Dylong said, turning to him. "What people?" His brow was lined.

"People like my brother. Like Paweł."

Dylong closed his hand and reduced the rock there to dust and let the dust filter between his fingers in four coarse streams. Then he slapped his palms against each other. "Time to go," he said. "They'll think we're starting another shift."

He stood up, brushed down his coveralls, and began gathering: pick, shovel, drill, drill bits, anthracite.

Gracian watched him, agitated. "Do you know something?" he said, trying to keep his voice steady, aware of the close edge of Dylong's temper. "Dylong, do you know something?"

And Dylong just buckled his canvas bag with the tin

and the drill bits inside and put it diagonally over him and swung the drill up over his shoulder, hoisting the shovel under the strap, and starting away toward the bend of the face where the roofless trains left for the lift shaft.

Gracian pushed himself up and ran after him, and though he was not much shorter than Dylong the boy felt half his size. He ran and overtook Dylong and stood himself firm in front of him, his arms poised, not knowing what to ready himself for. The boy could feel anger clenching his gut tight. Dylong looked at him.

"Get out of my way, Galileo," he said evenly.

"Please," the boy said, his voice low. "Please tell me what it is you know. About Paweł."

Dylong looked at him with grey eyes the colour of winter.

The anger had risen unexpectedly to the boy's throat and now it began to choke him. He could not find the words; his lips moved but no sound came. He felt his face darken. He stood there in front of Dylong, his mind racing.

"How can I earn my past when no one will tell it to me?" he said, finally.

"Ah. But it is not your past we speak of, is it?" Dylong said.

"But it is. It is, don't you see? My family. My past." He could say no more.

Dylong looked at him. He breathed loudly through his nose. He shifted the drill from one shoulder to the other. Finally he sighed.

"All right," he said.

They rode not speaking to the lift shaft, and the lift shuddered and then bored upward to ground, and they stepped out into light. They stopped the water flow in the carbide lamps and extinguished the lamps and then they walked to the equipment room and signed off the spare explosives and the drill and drill bits and went to the lockers. There were a few men there, loading up, and Dylong led the boy to a quiet place where rows of coats and jackets hung like shed skins and sat him down among them.

Dylong sat down opposite, glancing around warily as if he suspected ambush. He leaned forward, and the shadows of the hanging coattails on his face looked like the wings of bats.

"Now listen," he said. "Listen close, Galileo."

And Gracian listened. He listened to the silence

between Dylong's every breath as if that silence could yield to him a treasure unsurpassed. He became nothing but the act of listening, and such was the force of this transformation that Gracian felt that the very walls and the benches and the lockers and all about him listened too.

And then Dylong began.

✦

"It must have been eleven or twelve years ago. Those were difficult times for all of us—you probably can't even remember that far back, can you, Galileo?—but they were hard times, all right. Back then all the shops were full to bursting, that's true. Far cry from these starved days we're living now. But money was so scarce it didn't really make a shred of difference. And jobs, too. Jobs most of all. If you weren't already working you were in trouble. That's why every day I still thank God for the mines, and thank Him twice for the blessing of coal. Y'understand, Galileo? Because the first thing you've got to know about all this is that a man will do strange things when he can't get work.

"Twelve years ago. You were four years old, boy, nothing but a grub. Your father was alive. Your brother was about your age now, I suppose. A little older. A man, and full of a man's ignorance. Always was a strange creature, your brother. Had his own ways and stuck to them. Stubborn, afraid of company. But strong, a fighter, always getting into brawls, always riling people up in some way or another. Despite the quickness of his temper I don't think he asked for it, really. It just came to him.

"That was the time he began courting Anna Malewska, of course. And you can imagine, can't you, the number of other men, same age and older, too, he had to contend with? Some days they would come to his door just to ask to fight him and sometimes he'd come back bloodied, though more often he'd wipe the floor with them. Got quite a reputation for it, at so young an age. A real reputation. Still carries it with him in this village.

"But young Anna never loved him for that, Galileo. You see, Anna was always chiding him and slapping him about the head and making him blush for it. Anna's always been the only one who could keep the reins on him. No, she loved him for reasons all her own. Everyone could see she wouldn't even look at another man, despite everything she could have had from them. Despite her beauty. Not another single man. In truth it was Anna and Paweł together always, as if they were the very model of love, as if their names had been written together in the book of love. Or in the stars, eh, Galileo?

"Anyway, your brother had been learning leatherwork since he was fourteen or so, but all the trouble he got himself into and those own natural habits of his put him far out of favour with the man he was apprenticed to—old Manasik, who died a few years ago from too much vodka.

Manasik kept telling your brother to calm himself down or he would withdraw the apprenticeship with his shop, and what with so many men unemployed and what with him still living under your family's roof that would be a thing worth regretting for the rest of his life. Paweł was sixteen when Manasik started his threats. He put up with it for half a year, and then finally his patience crumbled just like coal under rotting brackets, and one afternoon he threw the saddle he was making half finished right at Manasik's belly, laying him to the floor. If he wasn't such a fat beast, I think he would have been crippled or even worse by the force of it.

"So Paweł left the leather trade.

"Thing is, Galileo, your mother and your father, they never knew of this. Francesca found out later, but she didn't tell them, didn't want to cause them upset. Your mother and your father only knew when it was too late. That's the next thing you have to understand about all this. Because Paweł told them he had left Manasik's employ, true enough, but then he also told them that a hidesman near Pietraszowice, your mother's birthplace, wanted his labour. This was a lie. This was the lie your brother told. And he worked hard and with great cunning to maintain that lie. You see, boy, Paweł did begin to work around Pietraszowice, but not in the way he told your family. And he came home the hours you would expect for a hardworking apprentice, often staying overnight on account of the travel distance. He made sure too that if your mother or your father had cared to make enquiries, a man who called himself Jorg Mroncz, bagmaker and saddlesmith, would vouch for him—as indeed

would many others, for Paweł had made a lot of connec-
tions where he needed them and made them fast.

"Now you must understand that Paweł did not start
this new venture all by himself. Even one such as Paweł
could not have the knowledge to do it, or necessarily the
will. To gain will, you must have others around prepared
to foster it in you. So this is what happened: After
Manasik kicked him out onto the street, Paweł fell in with
a bad crowd. Not from this village, mind you, but from
neighbouring parts. A wandering group of petty crimi-
nals and malingerers, Galileo, a no-good bunch. One or
two of them had heard of Paweł's troubles and had heard
too of his street brawls and his surly reputation. They
approached him, invited him to drink a bottle or two
of vodka and to smoke with them, and persuaded him
to join their team. And though great worry would be
brought upon your own family, boy, by your brother's
decision that day, if the truth be told I never really blamed
him for it. What could he do, without a job and a means to
help the family thrive? Unemployable—in this village,
anyway. Keen to keep Anna's love, and young; young and
filled with the heat of it in his blood. Perhaps I would
have done the same, Galileo, given the chance. For what is
crime but a darkened reflection of laws made to choke a
man? And it's always the young that get choked first.

"Have you guessed it yet, Galileo? I can see by that
gape of yours you have not. Then I will tell you: smuggling. Your brother became a smuggler. You should have
guessed it when I mentioned the land surrounding
Pietraszowice. Nothing but forests, forests as dense and
wild as those here in Maleńkowice. And to where do

those forests stretch? A good few kilometres into German soil, with no sure way to police the border there. There's just too much forest. But the smugglers had spent years learning the secret language of the trees and the brush, the tracks and trails that led through it and crossed the border into Germany. And Paweł too learned those paths and, so the story goes, learned them better than any of his fellow smugglers.

"Smuggling, Galileo, was no small trade back then. In that time of no work and little money in Poland and Germany alike, a good many farmers were willing to buy and exchange smuggled goods. The money you could make from smuggling was often less favourable than the payment in goods. There are things in Germany you can't easily get here, and it was the same the other way around. A certain type of German orange. A certain breed of Polish horse. So these things they smuggled. In and out across the border, through the forest. Paweł learned his craft quickly. He learned how to monitor the movements of the border guards who sometimes patrolled the German fields. Learned how to pick a single route through the forest and memorize it. Flashlights were easy giveaways, you see; better by far to run in darkness. And finally he learned always to enter and exit at the same point of the forest, or else you might get lost. And if you got lost, you got caught.

"I've heard tell that your brother smuggled entire herds of horses into Germany. With the other men he would ask the farmers who were known to them as allies to forsake any spare animals they might have in return for goods or money. Then, I'm afraid, they would swell the numbers by rustling from the farmers who wouldn't sell. Picking off an animal here and there where they had been allowed to roam abroad in the fields unsupervised, tossing their manes and blowing steam through their muzzles. And in the dead heart of the night they would lash the beasts together and ferry the whole lot through, stamping and blowing and rolling their eyes, straight into trucks waiting at the other end. That's quite something, eh, Galileo? Quite something.

"So all that time your mother and father believed he was working for the leathersmith, and he would bring back gifts of bags and purses to keep them believing. Fact is, boy, no parent wants to distrust a son. No parent wants the pain of such a discovery, no matter how strongly they suspect there is something to be discovered. So they believed, with or without the gifts, and Paweł continued his runs across the border. Eventually, of course, Francesca found out. She found two sacks of fresh oranges under his bed. She always was a bright girl, and curious too, curious like all the Sófkas seem to be, but Paweł made her promise not to tell and she agreed, not wanting trouble in the house.

"She must have worried, though. Because sometime later, I suppose after fretting and arguing it out in her head, she told Anna Malewska. And Anna was furious. None of us had ever seen such fury, though of course we didn't know then what stirred it in her. You should have seen her, marching through the village to the station! She went to Paweł that night and demanded he stop all his business with the smuggling, and stop it immediately.

"You see, Galileo, she was a bird keeper, and Paweł her

falcon. She let him fly now and then, and hunt and dive and create mischief abroad, but always only in a circle around her. And when she felt it was time she would draw the falcon back in, remind him whose care he was under and upon whom he relied. And then he would become as harmless as a common cockerel. Of every man in the village, Paweł understood this best. He knew his calling to her.

"And because of that young woman, that young man Paweł Sófka, barely older than you, remember, agreed to find another way to live. Perhaps if he had been quicker about it things would have continued harmlessly, with none offended. Who can tell with such things, like guessing the outcome of a rolling die? No one, not even me. Because Anna's pleas came only a few days too late.

"Paweł was already committed to one more night run through the forest, on the midnight between Saturday and Sunday. A small contraband, fruit and fish. He had given his word to the others, and you know Paweł is a man of his word. For Paweł, his word is his act; no gap exists between the two. Furthermore, if you ask me, he must have known full well then that to bow out of a smugglers' pact is like signing the warrant for your own death.

"Without telling Anna, he made what was to be his last illegal border crossing. Now, the way that team did it sometimes, especially with the smaller contrabands, was to divide the run between two men. One would take the goods halfway, meeting another man at the border point, often marked in the forest by only a few stakes, painted Polish colours on one side and German on the other, and sometimes even left unmarked. The second man would then finish the job. This is how it was arranged on this occasion. Paweł was to do the first part, the Polish run.

"And so he arrived at the forest at midnight, resolved to make this the last time he would come to this place. He carried two loaded sacks and a pistol. The route he would take was imprinted on his mind; if he closed his eyes he was already running it. On the stroke of midnight he began his trip. I dare say, Galileo, that he thought of many things as he ran—of Anna particularly, and of the new kind of life they might soon begin together. It would have been a warm night, despite the hour.

"Eventually he reached the rotted border stakes, bent in the earth by crawling tree roots. He had no light. The darkness of the forest whispered around him. And the second man was not there. Only empty night, waiting. Well, Paweł stood and waited too, growing nervous. Still the second man did not turn up. Paweł was just about to turn back, relieved, I'm sure, that nothing had happened, so nothing could go wrong, when he heard a noise coming from beyond the borderline on the German side. The noise came and then vanished and then came again. Paweł hesitated. He took one step into German territory. Then another and another. The noise seemed always ahead of him and he took more paces to follow it, always ready to run the short distance back to safety.

"And then from the darkness emerged men, three or four of them. Men with torches and guns, German police. Your brother turned around and saw more behind him. Trapped. No going back.

"Men whose business is deception often betray each

other. The second man had done just this. Perhaps he had got wind of Paweł's plans to quit the team and wished to punish him or cut him off before he became a dangerous liability. Perhaps he had simply made some deal with the German authorities. It is impossible to tell. Whatever the truth was, Paweł had no choice now but to run, ever further into German soil. He dropped the sacks and bolted, and the police gave chase. He sprinted until his lungs must have felt like bursting. Sprinted and sprinted. He knew much of the forest, which gave him the advantage. And he was fast, fast like a startled wild horse. He ran through the night and the torches grew smaller behind him. Then they started firing. Shots booming in the early morning darkness, Galileo, louder in that still forest than a dynamite charge in a coal face. Must have been quite a sound.

"But Paweł escaped them all. Nothing could touch him. Until finally he could run no more. Exhausted, he found the twisted overgrown stump of a tree and sat himself upon it. He could never have known for sure if he had lost his pursuers. Perhaps he even resigned himself to the possibility that his luck had run its course. Because the story is that Paweł didn't attempt to hide, didn't even attempt to keep moving. Just sat there, waiting for something to change. Perhaps he sat down as a way of saying to them, to everyone, 'Do with me what you will; there's no more left that I can give.'

"Occasionally he would hear a volley of shots echoing up from the trees. Gradually the volleys grew closer, and still he sat there. And then from nowhere a stray bullet, fired at random by one of the border patrol, found its target. It had been slowed by the foliage all around, you see, so when it hit Paweł it would hardly have moved him. It would have hit him gently, like a pin piercing a tyre: deflating him. It entered the left side of his chest and sneaked through a rib and grazed his lung. You've seen the scar there, haven't you, boy?"

He had; he had seen it! A thousand times he had seen it!

"They found him half an hour later, still sitting on the stump, one hand stemming the blood. He was arrested immediately. When the German police chief reached him, dragging his feet and wheezing from all the running, he stopped and unholstered his revolver. Then he pushed the catch and flipped open the chamber and tipped out one of the bullets. Held it up for Paweł to see, held it up reflecting the moon between his thumb and forefinger. Showed him what hit him.

"The rest? Well, the rest is a sad affair. Much of it you know or have seen, without knowing its true cause. Paweł was laid up in a hospital in Oppeln for three months and then thrown into Oppeln prison for another half year. When your parents found out they were truly shocked, I'm telling you. Your mother raged for weeks, wrote Paweł long letters about his disgrace, his betrayal of his family's trust. And your father—your father just seemed to close himself up, like a book you've lost interest in. You couldn't see inside him. He was still and solid, like brick. And sad. A sadness had him; he lost his fighter's strength. Your mother despaired at it. When the disease came on your father so soon after, a part of her, I think, blamed Paweł for his yielding to it. It shook your family at its heart, boy; I know you must have felt the vibrations. Any child with brains would have, and you've never been short of those.

"It must be said, though, that Anna Malewska did her best to argue Paweł's case, for she understood his predicament, despite his neglecting to tell her about that final job. She loved him, you see, and once love has been built, the foundations can take a lot of damage before they give way. At least that's my opinion. And I've known love.

"And Paweł? A change came over him in prison. He wrote letters back to his mother and to Anna, his lover, telling of his guilt and of his shame. He spoke of wanting to make amends, to find principle and structure in his life. When a man does not have structure, Galileo, his confidence in himself fades and falters. Each one of us needs a frame to hang ourselves upon, a frame of principles and notions and actions which we believe in. Otherwise we are simply baggy skins, empty ghosts of people. I think in prison young Paweł first realized this.

"He spoke of wanting to join the army. Or, rather, of the army as his last hope of gainful work. Of course, boy, this was not true. There are always employers here who are prepared to hire a young man with strength, and in any case the Polish authorities would have no real issue with Paweł after his release, since he was captured in Germany. But he got it into his head to join the army. Perhaps he thought he could find his frame there. He was seventeen years old, one year before he would have been called up for compulsory service.

"When he got out of Oppeln prison, he came home only to apologize to his family and to Anna. He poured his heart out to them. Hoped they would forgive him.

Then he travelled to the recruiting office in Katowice and lied about his age and signed the papers.

"They did forgive him, eventually, your mother and father, though the relationship between them all was never the same. A darkness slept always over them, casting its shadow. Anna was the only one to forgive him completely, forgive him as if nothing ever had happened.

"Paweł served in the Polish army for five years. By the time he left, your father had passed away. When he finally came back for good, his spirit had settled itself somewhat and he caused less trouble in the village. But there was an added intensity to him, a concentration of the old Paweł into something harder and sharper and more deep . . . within itself. He hardly spoke to the other villagers. He devoted himself to Anna. She became his fiancée and they lived together like monks, like hermits. In their own world. Then in 'thirty-eight he signed up again.

"But you know all this, Galileo; all this you know. And now you know it all. No one ever told you before because they believed what I have said to you already: The past is best left to the past. And let me tell you I feel cruel and like an idiot for telling you all this. But then you had to have it. You had to have it."

Finally, Dylong had finished. He sat and looked at Gracian, the bat-wing shadows flitting over his face.

"Is this all true?" Gracian said at last.

"As true as it could be."

"Are you sure? Did you see it with your own eyes? You couldn't have."

"I know everything that happens in this village. I told you; I am the eye that sees all." And Dylong's eyes were bright, but behind them shone a deep regretfulness.

"Now let's go," he said, "before someone takes us for conspirators and we end up in the camps. I tell you, boy, I don't know who's worse, the ones that invaded or the ones that've lived here all their lives."

Dylong stood. "This village has turned against itself, like a dog biting on its own tail."

With that, Dylong placed the flat of his hand on Gracian's back, and the boy stood, unable to feel his legs. He swayed once and steadied himself, pushing his hands into the coats. With his words, Dylong had forged a lens in the boy's head and peered down into it. Gracian felt a sense of invasion. He did not know what Dylong's story might bring; perhaps nothing would change, or perhaps a door had swung open, never to be closed again.

His head was reeling. He thought to himself, *The time is confused.* He thought to himself, *There's no knowing it.* He thought of Paweł's face and his mother's wooden spoon and the snow coming and then fading. He thought of Kukła's childlike pipe and Dylong's wide grin and the humming of heaters and the look in the eye of a German guard who had, on a day, let him pass: a look at once violent and furtive and knowing. He thought of the changes that had come over his own body. He thought of black sheets of coal, bruised eyes, telescopes, and the stars above, and he thought of Anna Malewska reaching up to touch her hair.

Three

✦

By the window in his room in his house, under an early morning sky high and wide and without cloud, stood the boy. His right hand held a simple crude telescope swinging slowly by his side, to and fro, to and fro.

The boy stood, and the telescope swung. Before him was his own reflection and beyond that was the darkened field and through the field ran the black form of the boy's brother, passing to the bottom and then vanishing. When the figure was no longer to be seen, the boy's eyes withdrew to his own face caught in the glass and withdrew still further until he saw the face of a young child.

The young child walked into his room, kicking his feet and swinging his arms and puffing his cheeks with air because he was bored. He walked up and down awhile and then began to run. He ran in wide circles around through the light slanting oblique across the room, his arms crooked out in front of him and making noises with his mouth. He was riding a galloping horse, because he liked the thought of riding a horse fast out along the land; he supposed he'd always liked the idea of escaping even now when he is a young child.

His brother rode horses. He did not see his brother often.

Soon the young child stopped galloping on his horse. He was bored again. He lay down on the floorboards and rested his chin on his elbow and then saw something in the corner of his eye. It was under his brother's bed. He crawled over to it, bored still but curious. It was a sack, made from material that was coarse and the colour of brick dust. He pulled on the sack and felt it was heavy. He had to get two hands on it and then pull it out, drag it out; his arms were too small, his hands were too small, but he could move it. Until it was there in front of him and he sat cross-legged on the floor looking at it. Then he reached forward and pulled it open.

Oranges. He couldn't believe his eyes. Round and fat, full of juice, and the colour of sunset. He plunged his arm inside just to feel them pack around it, then curled his hand about one he couldn't see and took it out. Then he peeled it, the pith jamming in his nails and the juice flowing down his wrist in rivulets. He ate. He ate another and then another. They were the sweetest he had tasted.

And now a figure stood in the doorway and he was caught there in his surprise, surrounded by slips of discarded peel, the flesh of an orange midway to his lips. It was his sister standing there. Her name was Francesca. Shamed, he proffered the uneaten fruit to her. She ignored it and concentrated on taking slow small steps toward him. Her eyes were wide and suspicious.

"What do you have there?" she was saying. "What do you have there?" and "Where did you find those?"

He pointed to where he had found them and Francesca got down on hands and knees and looked. There was another sack under the bed, which the young child reckoned was filled with oranges also, though he couldn't be sure.

Suddenly there was the noise of feet coming fast and heavy up the stairway, echoing, and the door swung wide and Paweł was there. And then Francesca standing up, so slowly, her eyes toward Paweł, not leaving his face, never leaving his face.

Gracian closed his eyes and saw again only the blankness and then opened his eyes. He tossed the telescope onto the bed behind him.

A frame. We need a frame to hang ourselves upon, he thought. He went to the chest of drawers and opened the first drawer and felt inside it and found his old penknife. With a nail he folded out the longest blade. Then he walked out of the room and into the narrow hallway and over to the window that Paweł had sealed shut a few months earlier.

And with the blade of the penknife in his fist he loosened the wood tacks a little, one by one.

It took him three nights of loosening, working only ten or fifteen minutes at a time to avoid the others finding him at it, before he could pull the tacks out with his bare fingers. When he had done this he went downstairs and waited till the kitchen was empty and opened the cupboard beneath the basin and took out a pointed tool used for marking screw holes from his father's old tool kit. He enlarged each of the holes made by the tacks in the wood of the frame by pushing in the marking tool and twisting it around. Then he reached into his pocket, took out the handful of tacks, and dropped them easily back into place, their flattened heads obscuring the widened holes.

Magic, Gracian whispered to himself when he had finished. *What looks real is really make-believe.*

Then he waited, until the rest of the house slept and

the stroke of midnight had come and gone again. He had put on his black trousers without a front button and tied about with a length of twine and also a black woollen sweater over a cocoa-brown shirt, which was the darkest he could find. His coat was blue but his hat and gloves and shoes were black. In the warmth of the house he sweated, but he did not care, for he was waiting, and when he had finished waiting he would sweat no more. The telescope had been pushed up the wide sleeve of his coat and lay uncomfortable against his arm like a splint.

When it was time he stood up, wiped the sweat away from the slope of his upper lip, and stepped out of his room.

At the end of the hall was a window. The moonlight painted pale oblongs onto the dirty wood. Downstairs slept his older sister and her husband and their baby.

He reached the window. He flipped the tacks out of their holes and caught them and pressed them into his pocket and undid the catch and eased the lower frame up as far as he needed.

The wood was old, and tiny white flakes tumbled down onto his hands.

He climbed out with an ease that was practiced, turned himself around on the ledge and knelt and gripped the wood, then lowered himself slowly until he was hanging by his fingers flat against the wall of the house. He reached out with one hand toward the crab-apple tree that grew in the yard—bare-branched now—and felt the rough cold bark of the nearest limb and held it tight. He gave a slight kick against the wall and then swung his other arm through space and clamped that hand around the branch. The snow exploded from the branches. He edged down the branch until he reached the trunk and then let himself fall onto solid ground.

He ran though the darkened yard, vaulting the wall there, across the rise of field beyond, and up toward the forest edge.

He guessed at the place at which he had seen Paweł enter the forest and went there and crouched in the thicket. He was some distance from the start of the route he used to take to the viewing place and could not tell what lay in the darkness beyond him. The patrol did not seem near. He let the telescope slip a little into the cup of his hand and cradled the narrower end, humming a tune to himself, a broken tune in a hum only he could hear. One of Morek's.

Góralu, czy ci nie żal . . .

He waited for a long time and his legs ached and his lower back too from crouching, but his head was clear still and his senses receptive. So that when a rustling and then a thin rushing of sound came from the rim of trees not more than fifty metres eastward, Gracian could move with a quickness. He scrambled forward some distance and then burst from the thicket and ran in a diagonal to the cover of a moss-shod tree and waited. A moment of silence and then a figure went before him. It was Paweł, passing swiftly.

Gracian turned and paused and then followed.

He kept Paweł always a safe distance in front of him, stopping occasionally to let it widen before moving on. To begin with he let the telescope fall into his waiting hand and swung it up to watch Paweł's movements. But to his disappointment he found that in the fluid darkness the lens was nearly useless. All it revealed was confusion, and in panic he almost lost his brother's tracks. He relied instead on his naked eyes, for although the night stretched itself into every corner, the moon brought light enough to make distinct forms of man and forest.

In this way Paweł led him, deeper and still deeper, into the tangled heart. And Gracian realized that he had entered a place unknown. He was no longer following but being drawn, for if he stopped now he might be lost to the forest.

They halted once at the sound of voices, both brothers closing the darkness around themselves and muting the rasps of their breaths. The patrol passed slowly through the space between them, two men with flashlights, and then was gone.

Sometime later Paweł stopped again, though there was no further sign of guards. It took the boy a moment to catch up, pushing himself behind a pine and lifting the telescope to his eye. Paweł was standing in a small clearing some way ahead, just visible against the bush. His back lifted up and down with the exertion of his breathing. Gracian settled himself, crouching among roots, one glove sucking up the damp earth. Silence spread out through the undergrowth. Still Paweł stood there, breathing.

Gracian heard a breaking of twigs by his ear and felt the presence of something close. A doe stood two feet away from him. Her body was strong and lean and her hide caught the moon along one side. She was standing with her legs planted, the front two twitching, bringing up a front hoof a little and placing it back down as if testing the ground. Her eyes were black stones with cores of light. They were looking straight at him. Steam was rising up from her. Then the doe flicked her neck and turned and was no longer there.

When Gracian looked again for Paweł he saw two of him. Instinctively he thought it must be a trick played by the forest; he lowered his gaze and rubbed his eyes and looked again. Where Paweł had been stood two figures, dressed alike in black. Was the other Anna? He thought perhaps it was, but now as he watched more figures emerged from the shadow, two of them, three, four. And then there were six there, six figures gesturing to each other, signing and then dispersing a little and running onward.

The boy stayed with them, behind them, not knowing what he should think about the sight that had gathered before him. The moonlight guided his way.

He was moving swiftly, muffled by the luminous snow, picking over roots and bracken. The forest passed around Gracian, back, beyond, branches reaching out but unable to sway such a progress, for it came from his feet and was drawn from energy and darkness, and his eyes streamed, and in every place was the smell of damp earth as the six figures led him on. Beneath his feet suddenly he felt a dipping of the land, a levelling, and saw the six figures move apart with precision from one another. And then emerging from between the sidelong trees, emerging as if heaving aside the forest, as if shrugging off the forest, was a cage of makeshift metal fencing and beyond that green sheet walls of aluminium, humps of outbuildings, two trucks low and heavy parked at an angle with their headlamps extinguished, sounds and forms enclosed and rising steam in the bitter cold, men moving, with rifles and without, spotlights punching through darkness like substitute suns casting raw outlined shadows on the white flat grass and catching silver on the fenced grilles.

The army base! The boy threw himself into cover and backed into a shallow leaf-clogged ditch. His body seemed then a conduit for an electricity blue and coursing. In his ears was a high-pitched resonance, like tapped crystal. Sweat slicked his brow and chilled instantly in the air, and his face was smeared with dirt.

If he lay down on his stomach in the ditch he could see the base rising beyond the undergrowth, and in that position he struggled to free the telescope from his sleeve and place it against his eye. The base perimeter glided back and forth in his vision.

Eventually he found three of the figures at the far edge by the trees where the fencing turned a corner. He could not tell if one was Paweł. The figures were crouched close to each other, looking into the base. One of them seemed to have a little notebook. He was writing in it and briefly consulting the others and then writing once more. They continued like this for some time.

On the flat of his belly, Gracian pushed himself nearer to the opening and lay still, watching. Then he moved slowly forward again until he reached the last bit of cover before the base fence. There he eased himself up and crouched and continued watching. The figures were not far away from him, seventy metres perhaps, still gathered at what seemed to be the far corner of the base. There was little activity inside the fence. There was only empty unlit ground for several hundred metres stretching between the fence and the hulk of an outbuilding. Now and again a guard would wander near the perimeter, rifle upslung, the shadows playing over him, and wander away.

There were a few soldiers here and there, talking or alone or smoking cigarettes. Many of the tents had no illumination. The entrance to the deep-grooved dirt track off which the trucks were parked lay almost directly opposite, and he could make out another unpaved road continuing into the forest. The entrance had been gated shut and bolted.

After a moment he saw the other three figures running nearly invisible among the shadows beyond the fence, past the edge of the nearest outbuilding. They stopped there and crouched down, and again one of them seemed to be taking notes in a notebook.

And now Gracian saw that one of the first three seemed to be moving ahead of the others, further beyond the fencing. Gracian moved through the bush, drawing nearer still.

The figure who had stepped forward was crouched, as if preparing for a jump. His head and shoulders were clearly visible now in the diffused light from the base, lifting out from the tree shadows like a spirit given form. The boy could make out the features of his brother.

A guard walked slowly into the open space behind the fence. He stopped, looked toward the forest. Gracian could see his brother and his brother could see the guard and he did not move even the slightest fraction. And then the guard looked away, distracted, readjusted the sling on his rifle, and made off again.

There was a pause of twenty breaths. Paweł tensed his

thighs and made a jump high onto the fence, gripping it and swinging himself like an athlete over and down onto the other side as if freed then of the bonds of gravity. When he hit the ground he sprinted to the cover of the outbuilding, merging with the long sweep of shadow cast there.

Gracian watched as Paweł moved round the inner perimeter, visible between the buildings. When he reached the third, he could just make out the edge of his body looking from behind the back sheet wall, surveying the scene. Then in an instant he had recrossed the fence and was talking again among the trees to the second group of three, outlining shapes with his hands and arms, and the figure with the notebook was writing quickly.

There was something more. A guard standing in that same empty stretch of ground into which Paweł had first jumped seemed to have stalled in his rounds and was standing staring out into the forest. He was looking in Gracian's direction, his mouth hanging open and his hands resting on the body of his rifle. He was stretching his neck and pointing his chin out and pushing his shoulders back and rocking on his boot heels.

Gracian shifted position, steadying the telescope. The guard looked at him.

And then Gracian saw a light.

The light was coming from his telescope. The lens was catching the dazzle of the arc lights and was marking him out as clearly as if it were a signal pulse he was himself sending to the world. In panic he lowered the telescope and collapsed it and crouched, unmoving. The guard was still looking, and with purpose now he took a step forward.

The forest waited.

A sound came from the guard's mouth—*Hey, Sie!*—and all of time and motion was unleashed like a blast. More cries came ringing and more arc lights lit up the forest, and Gracian turned and ran, swinging his head to see the six figures fleeing too. Now the cries were growing louder and a great whirl of noise seemed to break open the night, and then came a series of sounds more distinct, with edges clear and hard: the sounds of rifle cartridges expelled from barrels.

Fire and light and pressure. And those sounds echoed and multiplied and then something opened the air by his cheek and a section of tree bark before him exploded, and only then did he hear the whine of it, short and shrill, and then he was running and running and running and running.

For a time he did not know where he was running. But still he went on, stumbling over the uneven earth, twigs grazing his face and clawing his body. And then finally the forest edge was approaching and the sounds behind him were fading. He crossed out into the field, breaking from the forest's pull. Looking wildly above him as he ran, the boy saw that the stars were thin white streams connecting, a beautiful alphabet in the sky.

He slept a few hours that night and only then because his body begged for rest. He writhed and bridled in his bed and his mind was overrun by nightmares. He dreamed of six black dogs with red eyes chasing him and of his brother eaten whole by shadows.

When he awoke he was at the very edge of the bed, sweating and breathing shallowly. Opening his eyes he saw on the floor below him his book, *Wstęp Do Astronomii,* open at the last page he had read, a yellow plane in the sunlight.

Constellation Gemini. A tale of two brothers, the constellation of his birth. A picture there of fifteen stars, one for each year of his life.

His mother was in the kitchen reading a German newspaper through the spectacles that he hardly ever saw her wear. She was frowning as she read. Józef Kukła was there also, readying to leave for the bakery. To the boy everything about the room seemed suspicious.

"Hello, Gracian," his mother said. "You look terrible this morning. Look at how black your eyes are."

Gracian buttoned his coat and tied his hat on. He picked up his lamp, which stood against the wall below the three empty coat hooks and the figure of Christ crucified, and opened the small hatch in the lamp base and checked the carbide, the smell as always repulsing him. Then he made for the door.

"Eat something," his mother said.

"I'm late," he said. "I have to go." At the door he stopped. "Have you seen Paweł today?" he said.

There was a pause.

"What kind of a question is that?" said Józef Kukła.

Outside, the snow was lying in drifts. He made his way up the main street toward the colliery. People walked the streets just as they always did. The sun was white and smeared across the sky but still bright. He noticed that the coal dust in the air was a little heavier than usual. When he was nearly at the colliery gates, Gracian began to shiver. Soon his whole body was shaking uncontrollably and his teeth chattered and the sickness rose sour in his throat. He fell upon one knee onto the cobbles and clenched his fists and squeezed his eyes shut. The snow dust moted round him. The shivers passed. He got up and walked on.

At two o'clock he emerged from the mine, offloaded the equipment, and headed for home. The events of the previous night seemed now to have lost some effect, their memory flattened out like a scene on a picture postcard. If it were not for the sense of dread he felt rising in him, the boy might have persuaded himself they had never occurred. He crossed the road when he reached the shop that was once a confectioner's and was now a makeshift post office with shutters halfway down the windows so they looked like drowsy eyes. As he did so, he caught in the edges of his vision another man crossing behind him.

He glanced back and saw that the man was dressed in dark green with a dark overcoat with the collar up, and Gracian recognized him as one of the *Schupo*. He was walking slowly with his hands dug down into his coat pockets. He had a short precise gait but with a languid rolling of the shoulders. His face was impassive. Gracian quickened his progress along the street and in a short while became aware that a second *Schupo* was on the other side of the road, a little ahead of the other, keeping step. The second *Schupo,* too, did not look at him.

There were other villagers passing by, some in conversation and others not, some passing slowly and others fast, but the two *Schupo* did not pay them any heed. They kept pace with Gracian, quickening when he quickened, slowing when he slowed, always some strides behind him, down the main street.

He stopped walking in the direction of his home. Instead he turned down a narrow bystreet that led between two buildings and had not been gritted, so the snow was tamped down to a translucent crust laced black with dirt. He moved swiftly along until the street opened out a little and there were houses to the left and right of him. He knew who lived in those houses; he had known the faces of the occupants for all his life. In a village, so they said, no one is a stranger. He thought of knocking on one of the doors. He looked back at the street; the passing of people on the main street could just be seen. The two *Schupo*s had not followed him.

He lingered where he was in the snow. The street was empty. He swung the carbide lamp, gripped by its thin metal hanger, lightly by his side. His eyes burned and he rubbed them with the back of his free hand. The coal dust was bad today.

Then the two *Schupo*s turned into the narrow street. They were side by side, blocking the passage. They walked quickly. He turned away from them and saw two more *Schupo*s coming toward him.

Behind was clear street, but he did not move. He did not believe he could outrun them.

He stood looking at their faces as they approached him. Now two stood in front of him, and the other two behind. One of those in front, the tallest, with a smooth youthful face whose cheeks had blotched rose-petal pink in the cold, was smiling and clapping his leather-gloved hands together with a noise that reverberated. Gracian looked at the snow on the *Schupo*'s shoulders.

"Are you Sófka," he said, in a way that was not a question.

Gracian looked at the four of them. Their gazes were like walls.

"Why?" he said.

The tallest one let out a staccato laugh. "That's not a question you should ask us," he said.

His skin was so smooth and pale. Hardly older than Gracian. They were all boys together.

"We have a message for you," the tallest one said.

Gracian did not reply.

"Did you hear me, Sófka? A message. For you. Don't you want to know it?"

Still he kept silent.

The tallest one made a gesture with his chin at one of the two behind him, and Gracian turned a little toward him.

"Tell him the message," the tallest one said.

The one who stepped forward was wider of build and with a bullish face and neck, and his lower lip protruded with the aspect of a sulking child. He seemed serious, wrapped in concentration. He stepped forward and took off his hat and threw it down into the snow. Then he slowly removed his gloves and tossed them into the cradle of the hat. He made his hands into fists and stepped toward Gracian.

In one movement Gracian swung the carbide lamp up and round and into his face. He felt the force of it tear one end of the handle from its bracket and when he brought it down the lamp hung at a strange angle from the wire strip. The *Schupo* was leaning over to one side. There was blood coming from his face. He remained this way for a moment and then staggered and fell onto the cobbles, clutching at his cheek.

Another rounded on Gracian and he tried again to raise the lamp but he had no grip on it now, and someone kicked it from his fingers and he saw the lump of carbide fly from the lamp base and skip across the ground and then someone else hit him square in the stomach. He folded over, though he was still standing. But the blows were coming from all sides, and it was hard to block them, and then he was down in the snow.

As they beat him he thought of the viewing place, of the smell of the earth there and the silence of it. He made no noise other than when air was forced from his lungs.

Eventually they tired and stepped back from him. He squinted upward and saw the tallest one panting, his cheeks now a different red, hat askew on his head. He straightened it and wiped a hand across his neck, his chin. He straightened his coat. The *Schupo* he had struck with the lamp stood behind, blood welling at his temple.

"The message," the tallest one said, breathless, "is this, Sófka. Tell your brother we will get him. Tell him that we know what he's up to and that we will let him wait and then we'll make him suffer in ways he could not imagine."

He kicked Gracian in his belly twice, one for each of his parting words.

"Got . . . that?"

Lying with his eyes closed and knees drawn up, it took the boy some time to realize they had gone. One of his eyes seemed to have swelled and he could see little through it. The gaze of the other now rested upon the cobblestones.

Their edges rose from the snow bed like gentle mountains, sheened in the dimming light. At the rim of sight loomed the broken lamp, with the carbide fragment a distance from it, like a treasure torn from a shipwreck. He could taste blood in his mouth.

Slowly and with great deliberation he pushed himself onto his elbows, then hands, then knees, and stood up. He could not straighten himself out fully. There was a noise like running water in his ears. He took a step and felt nauseated and waited and stepped forward again. There was pain all over the surface of him, his skin leaping at the touch of air. He made his way slowly over to the lamp and scooped the carbide up and back into the lower compartment. The handle was broken but could be fixed. The reflector was intact, as was the water valve. Light could still be had from it. He thought suddenly of walking through an empty mine shaft among endless lamplight constellations.

As he made his way home, he did not know how long he took or how he was moving his body. Once or twice he looked down and saw bright drops of blood soaking into the snow. Blooming there, like the crimson flowers by the river Hron.

Gracian reached the house and sat down on the thin stone step below the door. He leaned his back against the wooden door slats and stared into space. Every so often he lifted one hand up behind him and knocked faintly, with what strength he had, upon the door.

After a time he heard noises inside and felt a vibration pass through the door and then it was opened. He fell a little and brought a hand down on the stone to support himself, tipping his head back. His mother stood over him.

"Gracian! You too! This is too much! God help us, oh!" she said. She bent down and put her hands under his arms and lifted him, and then he passed out.

He came to a few minutes later. He was seated on a chair pushed up against the wall of the kitchen by the door. His mother was bending over him with a tin bowl of water and a rag and was wiping his face. He could see other figures indistinct behind her. As his mother dabbed at him he turned his head a little from one side to the other, feeling the cool water come down over the rise of his cheeks and across his lips. His mouth was opening and closing. "I think we've saved it," he kept saying, "I think we've saved it. We can still see."

After a short while Gracian stopped turning his head and speaking strange words. His eyes opened wider and he returned from wherever it was he had been. He could see his mother clearly, though the room behind still shifted and wavered, and he could see the details of her round face as she tended him. Her dark eyes had a circling of red around them and her face was drawn, the cheeks sagging and the lines from her nose deep and heavy. Her hair, pulled back, had broken in places from its binding and strands leaped up from her head to make abstract blurs against the dimming light. When she looked at him her eyes were active, searching, fragile.

"What's wrong?" he said, smarting at the cuts around his mouth.

He was aware of a movement behind them and the movement was a door opening and someone walking through into the room, head bowed, looking up toward Gracian and shouting, "Bastards! *Bękarty!*" Then two people whom he recognized as his sister and Józef Kukła holding the person back, calming him, speaking in low voices, stroking his back.

"*Gracian,*" the person said, and he knew it was Paweł.

"What's wrong?" Gracian said, pushing away his

mother's hand and the wet rag in it, leaning forward in his chair, wincing. "What's wrong?"

She looked at him with her restless eyes. "There has been great tragedy today, Gracian my darling," she said in a soft voice, a voice he remembered from childhood.

"Let me see," he said. "Let me see!"

She lowered her head and rose and moved aside for him.

Next to the kitchen table was a tableau of three figures. His brother was between Francesca and Józef Kukła, bent forward where he stood, his damaged hand prominent, covering his face, and the other clutching at his hair. His body seemed to vibrate, and Francesca and Kukła stood over him, their hands light on his shoulders, his back, soothing.

On the kitchen table a woman was laid out. She was dressed all in black and her face rose from it, so pale and alight as to be the impassive mask of a *Święta* Maria. Her hair spread out away from her cheeks across the table, falling in one smooth long stroke beneath the table edge.

Without speaking and without anyone moving either to help or hinder him, Gracian rose and walked to the woman, no longer feeling the weight of his body. He stood over her. He lifted his hand and held it palm down a few inches from her stilled face and then moved it over her until it reached the small red hole in the centre of her chest, where the bullet had left her body. With his hand he covered the hole from his eyes and moved his palm back up to her face and brought it down again to his side. He saw now that a dark line of concern had blended with her beauty. There were two thin creases lifting vertically from the clear space between her eyebrows, and her lips, though still the pink of dusk, and full, were pressed together tightly. Her eyes were open. A film of light had covered them, dulling their colour. Anna Malewska's eyes looked like two distant planets, turning no more.

✦

In the minutes and hours that followed, Gracian sat on his chair as a theatre of moving faces passed before him. With soft caressing words, in the kitchen with its darkly burdened table floating between the silver pans, his mother explained to him that the previous night Paweł and Anna had been seen by German soldiers in the forest after curfew and that, while fleeing, Anna had caught a bullet and the wound had proved fatal. Paweł had hidden with her huddled beside him until late morning, when he returned, bearing her lifeless body to the house.

The others listened with closed faces as Gracian was told this news, and his eyes moved from one to the other: Francesca with her long hair down, Józef Kukła's high cheekbones, Paweł. Gracian saw then that the lives of the people in this room would be connected always by an indissoluble bond, and the shape of that bond lay silent and in black upon the table. The five of them had become points frozen into a new constellation. And the constellation was upon the earth, and the story it told was one of death.

When Gracian had asked the question burning to leave his lips, What had they been doing there, so late, in the forest? his mother had smiled and come to him with more water for his face and hands and told him not to worry himself; he should rest for the bruises to heal.

At this, Paweł had looked up from where he had been kneeling at the table end, his hands around the feet of Anna Malewska and his forehead pressed against the soles. He looked up and said, "Enough, Mother," in a voice that seemed dredged from some lived dream. "There's nothing to keep from him." His eyes were indistinct and yet directed at Gracian. "An army of people is rising," he said, "all over this country. A net is spreading, at the word of President Raczkiewicz and General Sikorski in London, cast by ourselves in villages and towns and cities, to trap the German army. Last night in the forest we were collecting intelligence for the spreading of that net; it's called reconnaissance, do you see, brother?" And then his face seemed to crumple, disintegrate, and he looked at his hands, turning them over as if he'd never seen them before, and his voice sounded broken. "But last night I was sure of myself," he said, "and now I do not know what to do. I am lost." He turned to their mother, with his three-fingered hand stretching out in a soundless plea.

Gracian had watched as his mother drew herself up,

became large, larger, growing in the centre of the room. Her shadow lengthened, and the power she had was the power of her temperament, for always she had been organizer, orderer of events, corrector; and as she spoke now her sons, her daughter, and her daughter's husband nodded and obeyed, for her voice was commanding.

"We shall stay with her tonight," she said. "From what you have told me, Paweł, the Germans have no reason to suspect that any one of you was shot?"

"True."

"And do the other ones know about Anna?"

"No."

"And her mother and father, the Malewskas, do they know of your involvement?"

"Yes."

"Can they be trusted?"

"Yes. They have often assisted us in their way."

"Then I will tell them tonight and you will tell those others that you can, and tomorrow we shall take her out into the fields and bury her. She will not be denied that. But there must only be a few of us. Gracian and I shall go to the mine early tomorrow. We'll say he had a bad fall and ask for a few days' rest. They should give us that, *Boska Wola,* God willing. And Paweł, my son, you realize that you must go to work in the morning. We cannot give them any reason to suspect. Go to work and afterward meet us at the place of the burial."

"Yes, Mother."

"We will spread the news that Anna Malewska has disappeared. Vanished. Taken, perhaps, into Germany. There is no other choice. It is our best hope."

Then she pointed her finger at those who listened, drawing it round in an arc as if to link them together. Her voice was solemn.

"What has happened here must forever remain secret. Not a word must be spoken to anyone else. For the good of us all, no one else will know about Anna. Is that understood?"

And each of them in turn said yes, for they understood well enough.

The funeral was held in the early afternoon in a deserted field some way from Maleńkowice. It lasted only a little time. Apart from the family there were William and Urszula Malewska, their faces red and stricken, and four others, whom Gracian supposed were the figures he had seen in the forest. They stood around the opened ground in a broken ring. When Paweł arrived from Osok, one of the men gave a service and Anna Malewska was lowered into the waiting earth. The wind was strong and the snow eddied, the clothes of the watchers whipped and billowed.

Gracian could barely stand. His lips were swollen and his cheek too, and his skin bore patches of yellow and violet. It was painful for him to watch, and the pain was not only without but also within, a chattering of voices. When the earth had been shovelled back on her and the tamped mound marked by a tiny cross, those present dispersed slowly into the field. Paweł turned and his face was pale, without blood, and Gracian, who had stood some way from the others, lifted his eyes to the wide grey horizon. A flock of birds twisted through the distant sky.

Paweł saw his mother then. After a moment she opened her arms and he sank down between them, his cheek to her breast. "I just wanted to keep us all together. That's all I asked for," Gracian heard his mother say, her voice dipping on the wind.

He turned to look, but Paweł had become only a pair of arms around his mother's back, his hands gripping her coat there, knuckles showing white.

When guilt is serious it grows in stages, like the winter. First is the creeping ground frost, spreading out across the mind yet leaving the space still for old roots of doubt and debate to breathe, and with them the seeds of absolution. Perhaps it was not he who had alerted the guards? Perhaps they would always have been caught, if not then at least eventually? And could he control the wanderings of light? Or the path of a bullet? Hadn't Paweł given him the telescope in the first place? And how did he ever get hold of it? But such questions soon become exhausting, and then the air hardens and the ice congeals and there is no turning away. Guilt has taken over and remains.

So it was for Gracian Sófka, lying each night beside his brother, his outer wounds fading slowly and sleep rarely claiming him. Occasionally in the day he would be struck again by an attack of shivering, his very toes and finger-tips shaking and then finally calming. He felt there was something growing inside him, bursting to escape, trembling, making him tremble with it. He lay awake and watched his brother—restless, sometimes weeping in his sleep—and felt it wanting to flow out in one long stream through his lips and relieve him of its pressure. But he could not bring himself to let it. He feared it, and the release of it, and what that might bring.

Thus the brothers were once again united. Gracian's mother had taken him to the foreman of colliery Richter, Herr Schultz, who sat with his long unhumorous face behind a small desk in the little office with green stone walls cold to the touch. He wore glasses, over which he regarded the boy and mother before him, the boy with heavy bruises and his hands raw, the mother making his plea. Ridiculous, it was clear Schultz had thought. The boy should state his own case. He's old enough. The fore-man's lips were narrow and pale and not the kind that parted easily with words, and when finally they opened it was to give out seven of them: "Four days, I can do no more."

Paweł continued to work, forcing himself awake long before the break of day for the walk to Osok. When he came home it was as if he were his own empty reflection. No emotion passed across his features, and the blankness of his eyes was the blankness of grief. His mother treated him tenderly, taking food up to him where he would sit in the brothers' room or sometimes lie on the bed, his hands crossed upon his chest. Even Kukła seemed shocked by Paweł's state and would now and then mutter a consolation, his eyes downcast. In such a condition it was harder than ever for Gracian to speak with his brother.

But a night came on the final day of Gracian's convalescence. The brothers had been lying beside each other in silence for some time, and in the play of darkness the space between their beds seemed depthless. Neither slept. Gracian lay and listened to each rough nuance of sound, the pressure ebbing and thickening in his throat. He felt the presence of something weighted in the air. Then there was a shifting of springs and falling fabric from his brother's bed and a lamp sparked, slicing yellow light through the room.

Paweł was turned toward him in his bed. He seemed suddenly anxious, eager. "How's the telescope, Gracian?" he said.

Gracian did not move. He lay facing upward, able in the gold light to see the smooth high ceiling.

"The telescope," Paweł said again. "Have you been using it?"

"A little."

"A little? Why not a lot?" Paweł was sitting up now, his legs half swung across the mattress edge. "Can I see it?"

"Why?"

"I want to see it."

Gracian moved with difficulty, until he could reach below his own bed. He found the place in which he had concealed the telescope and pulled it out. Paweł held out his hand but the boy did not give it to him. He felt shivers rising and quelled them, his eyes shut.

"Give it," Paweł said.

And reluctantly he gave it over.

Paweł turned the telescope in his hands. The lamplight caught on its curvature, and a thin arc of brightness fell over Paweł's face. He was smiling.

"Beautiful, isn't it? I just wanted to look at it. It was my present to you. I wanted you to get some use from it," he said, leaning back a little, scratching at his chin. He was unshaven.

He ran his fingers over the telescope, retracted and extended it once more. Then he lifted it to his eye and looked through the wide end into the obscurity of the room.

Gracian was up now, watching. As Paweł turned his head, the telescope tapered away from his head like a watch mender's loupe but grown gigantic, ugly.

"I've never looked through that end," Gracian said.

When Paweł brought the telescope down, his smile had gone. "No?" he said. "Perhaps you should, one day. Makes everything simpler, you see. Just a small clear picture."

The words wrapped themselves around Gracian's heart. He made a gesture with his hand as if to illustrate something he had not said. He sat forward, looked into Paweł's eyes.

"How," Gracian said then, "can we be certain of things?"

Paweł looked at the boy. There was longing in his expression. After several moments he handed the telescope back to him and pushed himself forward until his feet were firm upon the floor and sat straight opposite him, less than three hands' breadth separating their faces.

"This is a time of choices, brother," Paweł said. "Anna

made hers, and I made mine. We made our choices together. That is all we have in this world. We live by choices, and we die by them."

Then he let a sound out through his nose and stared down at his feet. Slowly, and after some time, he tilted his head, as if to ask *What?*

Gracian could hear him breathing.

"She was all that I was, Gracian," he said, and there were tears on his face, "and she was more than that too. How can I do without her?"

Paweł leaned over suddenly, reached across and put out the lamp. He lay back in the dark upon his bed. No sound came from him, not even breath. After a time Gracian felt he could speak. He was fearful.

"The men," he said. "The *Schupos*. They told me they were going to get you. Hurt you. They said to give you that message. That they knew."

He heard Paweł move over the covers.

"It's all right, Gracian," his brother said in the quiet. "Someone will get me sooner or later. I'm not afraid of it. From the beginning, that has been my destiny."

And as the shivers came back to Gracian, swimming quickly up through his body, flowing down into his arms and fingers, the image entered his mind and lingered: a dress draped over a chair back in an empty room, two small shoes below it, both pointing a little sideward, as if soon to begin a journey of their own.

✦

The conversation remained in Gracian's thoughts. He went back to work at the colliery, even though still his skin had not healed and the cuts on his limbs made it difficult to dig.

"Those *beasts*," Dylong said, his voice a low sharp hiss, huge arms straining beneath the sleeves. "If I could I'd pick them off one by one. How dare they do this to Galileo—my trusted partner?"

Once he asked about Anna Malewska, drawing Gracian aside and speaking low under his breath.

"Any news of her? The village is talking, yabbering; the story is she's gone, simply vanished. Paweł must be sick with the worry." He moved in closer, his breath heated. "We all fear the worst."

To this Gracian did not reply.

————

Two weeks after Anna's death, Gracian awoke in the early hours drenched in sweat. Paweł slept next to him, muttering in his slumbers. Gracian lay very still and then eased himself out of bed. The brick heater had been baking all night and the room was very warm. He wore only a loose shirt and long underwear. Taking care not to disturb his brother, he walked, up on his toes, across the room. He reached the window and pulled it down slowly, the glass rattling with a light keen noise that belonged to another—sunlit—world.

Gracian's thoughts had turned again, inexorably, to the stars. He had been too weak and the shivers had come too often recently for him to pay them heed. But as the days passed, he had felt their attraction return. He saw them when he closed his eyes, strewn across that private darkness, speeding his heart.

Now they were laid out before him in the cloudless sky. Gracian gazed at them all, hundreds of them, more finding his eyes the more he gazed. The desperation was upon him. He felt it contorting his face, pulling down the edges of his mouth, and congesting his chest. Breath clogged his throat.

He stretched out his hands then, out of the open window, reached them out toward the stars. Among them, he knew, there was never loneliness, for they had known nothing but solitude. No time, for they had known nothing but the slow burn of millennia. No happiness and no sadness and no responsibility, for they had known nothing but the silence. Since he was a child he had come to them for release from all around him. Now he asked them for what they had always given him. He asked them not with words but with the shivers of his body, his hands outstretched. He asked them to relinquish, to advise, instruct, listen. He fought to rise up to them.

But they would not have him. High above they shone, mute and cold and resolute. And at that moment, Gracian could make out nothing within them that might be deemed human.

He recoiled from the window and sat down below it, his back to the wall, the open glass above him. He covered his face with his palms and let out dry sobs, devoid of tears.

It was then, sitting below the window with his back to the stars, that Gracian made a decision. At first it was like a gas, but then it took on shape until it filled him up hard and solid. Tomorrow he would go to his brother and he would tell him. He would present to him the truth. About Anna, about everything else. Each word of it. And he would not stop until the telling was done.

✦

Since Paweł had caught him in the viewing place, less than half a year had elapsed. Old Man Morek sang no more; his season had ended. The war had entered its second year.

Perhaps, in their journey, the stars throw invisible shadows upon the earth.

The decision stayed with Gracian and grew in strength until it possessed him like a fever. He planned to tell Paweł the next day, after he returned from the mine. He reached home and moved swiftly through each room of the lower house and then each room of the upper. Paweł was nowhere to be seen.

He found his mother and asked her, "Where is Paweł?"

She regarded him. "Didn't he tell you? Paweł has gone

to stay with William and Urszula. He wanted to see them, to be in the apartment. There are memories there for him."

"What?" Gracian said, shocked. "When will he be back?"

"In a few days. Two days, I think."

"But surely it's not safe for him there—"

"Safe there as here, Gracian. I think now we should let him be." She nodded hard, confirming her own words. "He'll be back."

Gracian left the house and walked quickly in the direction of the Malewskas' flat. But once again he was unable to complete the trip. Standing in the street, he imagined himself knocking on the door of the apartment and bringing to it a new dimension of sadness. It should not be that way, he thought. Paweł would return in two days. He stopped where he was and turned back home again.

But the next morning there was a collapse at colliery Osok. Pressure that had built up slowly and unchecked in the rocks took the moment to expend itself. One hundred and seventeen square metres of coal and rock gave way, splintering the roof slats. Paweł had been shovelling out rock when it happened, leaning on his side in the crevice of a metre-high face, the walls close around him and the ceiling low over his head. His partner worked below, his boots braced against the wall. They were alerted first by a rain of soot, so fine as to be the touch of a gentle breeze. Then a sound like tearing, the lamps flickering.

Paweł was not far from the site of the collapse. When it came he looked upward and opened his mouth, as if to call the earth down upon him. Blackness lined his throat, filled his lungs. He reached out with his hands, and the rock swallowed him.

The dust cloud roiled and thundered through the mine, churning outward with its own black life. It reached as far as the lift shaft, half choking the men there. On the surface was felt a gentle vibration, and for the briefest moment a shimmering band of movement swept over the streets of Osok.

It took some hours for the colliery officials and surviving miners to ascertain the extent of the damage. The lifts would not work properly and had to be fixed. Sparse clouds of coal dust spiralled languidly around the shaft opening. The few inhabitants of Osok gathered around the colliery building, and a great hum of voices rose up from them. By and by it was found that fourteen men had lost their lives.

In the late afternoon a man from the colliery made the walk to Maleńkowice to inform the family. Gracian had returned from colliery Richter and stood at the top of the stairs when he heard the door open. The man wore a blue suit that didn't fit him and had removed his tie and stuffed it into one pocket so the top folded out like a dark tongue. There was dirt on his face and hands.

The man told them where he had come from, and Gracian's mother did not have to hear him speak further. She looked at his face, his old suit, and began to wail. She moved unsteadily around the kitchen, shouting and weeping, until she caught hold of Francesca, and both women went down onto the floor together, the younger supporting her mother. Gracian remained where he was, at the top of the stairs. Józef Kukła was still working.

When their mother was a little calmer, the man from the colliery told them what had happened. When he had finished he said, "I'll leave you alone," and closed the front door softly, as if not to wake a child.

In the evening Gerard Dylong came to visit them. He stood in the doorway, his head nearly touching the frame top. His hat was in his hands, and his hands hung unsure over his chest. Gracian watched his entrance from his vantage at the top of the stairs. He saw Dylong talking to his mother, putting his hand on her shoulder, and then his mother shaking her head and thanking him and leaving the room. He saw Dylong talk next with Francesca, for a longer time, Francesca standing with one hand on her hip and the other arm cradling the sleeping baby, every so often brushing hair away from her face. One of Dylong's fingers was the length of the baby's head. Some of their talk came up to Gracian. He heard Dylong say "sudden" and "proud" and "It really is a riddle." And once he heard his sister say, "In a way I suppose it's a mercy. I was afraid he'd die . . . by other means. Worse ones."

Then Dylong said something and Francesca pointed to the ceiling, and Dylong made his way toward the stairs.

Dylong found the boy in his room. He was sitting on the floor below the window, which had been opened wide. The room was full of cold air.

"Hello, Galileo," he said, stooping a little, his hat still clutched like a scrap.

When the boy did not answer, Dylong took a few steps forward, hesitant, and sat himself upon the corner of the far bed.

"I just came here to check up on my partner."

The boy's eyes were on the wall.

"I have a friend who works at Osok. He said the collapse happened quick and heavy, in the blink of an eye. Anyone trapped wouldn't have felt a thing," Dylong said. "Coal's like that, rough and gentle by measures."

The boy had closed his eyes. Dylong ran the back of his hand over his mouth, played with the fraying stitches of his hat.

"I'm sorry, boy," he said. Then he stood up. "I'm going now." He made toward the door, then spoke again.

"Remember, we've got sulphur to look for. I need you for that. We'll find it yet. I'm telling you, we'll find it." Again, he broke off. When he reached the door he turned and put his hat on.

"I know people say I'm deranged," Dylong said then, quietly. "And it's true that even if I did find the sulphur, it probably wouldn't be me who'd profit from it." He tapped his finger once against his forehead. "But if you spend your life digging through coal, you better have a good reason." He smiled a sad smile and made again to leave. "See you soon, Galileo."

"Dylong."

"Yes?"

"Why do you always call me by that name?"

Dylong looked at Gracian and Gracian looked back at Dylong.

"Because you're a star-gazer, boy," Dylong said. "You always will be—even if tomorrow the stars fell out of the sky."

Later Gracian opened his eyes and realized he had slipped into sleep. Outside, night had fallen. He stood up slowly and began to pace up and down. On his seventh circuit of the room he vomited liquid in the corner by the door. He knelt down, wiping at his mouth until the nausea stopped. Then he looked up and saw the two empty beds, and in a rage he set upon them. He pulled off the linen and trod on it with his boots. He tipped the mattresses from their iron harnesses and tried to tear them. He broke most of the metal springs. Afterward he went to the wardrobe and threw the clothes out onto the floor, and the hangers also. He splintered the wood with his fists, his feet. Then for a long time he sat in the wreckage of the wardrobe and looked at nothing. For a moment something had seethed, but now it had gone. He felt helpless.

Gradually, however, sitting among the twisted hangers

and shards of wood, a clarity entered him. He felt a convergence, a resolution. An immense weight had dissolved; the world felt lighter. He put on his coat and gloves and hat and gathered that which he needed, tucking it all down into the coat folds. Then he went downstairs.

They sat around the kitchen table in silence. Gracian did not know when they had arrived there or if they had heard the noise coming from his room. When he appeared at the door, his mother glanced up.

"Gracian, it's you. I think I must have been sleeping. How are you?" She looked him up and down. "Where are you going?" she said.

"I won't be long."

"But curfew's nearly fallen."

"I have to go. I won't be long," Gracian said.

"Gracian, no—"

He went over to his mother and embraced her, smelled her fragrance, stroked her hair.

"Oh," she said, pressing her face into his neck, beginning to weep. "It's too much," she said.

"I know," Gracian said.

"I am partly responsible, I know I am," his mother said through the weeping, her face ruined. "I asked him to get that job."

Gracian looked down at her, at the top of her head. "He didn't do that for you, Mother," he said.

Looking up then, she saw great kindness in her young son's face.

And when he walked through the door, nobody tried to stop him.

And so Gracian made his final journey into the forest. After a time he reached the viewing place. It was just as he had remembered it. As if this little piece of the world had been waiting for his return all along. He had forgotten the beauty of it: the trees piling up toward the sky, the concentration of silence, the silver wash of moonlight. Snow covered the ground, the tips of the grass and the hide of moss showing through.

He walked slowly around the small clearing and then tipped his head back. Tonight the forest gave out a kind of glow, a soft cradle for the stars. Gracian walked into the centre of the viewing place and reached into his coat and removed the book, faded red letters on cream, and the telescope. He held one in each palm and looked at them.

His breaths were ragged bursts. Colour had blossomed

in his cheeks and his eyelids fluttered, the wings of butterflies. He lowered himself to his knees and placed the book and the telescope on the earth before him. Then he stood and took off his gloves and pushed them into his pocket. He lifted his head once more and saw the constellations set in their places.

The stars can wait, Paweł had said. *That's all they ever do.* And he knew this to be true. The stars would wait, wait and watch, but no longer would he watch them. For his life was not theirs, and his flesh was not that of gas and fire. His flesh was real and the last and truest boundary, and now he felt against it tiny far-spaced pricklings, growing quicker. He looked down beneath him and saw round dark dents sink into the snow, and these shallows became deeper and more scattered, and then it was raining, long heavy drops tumbling, splashing onto his skin.

There was a swelling in his veins. The rain was falling, washing off the snow, and he knew that winter had finally passed. Gracian went down again onto his knees in the centre of the viewing place, water running down his face, water washing the earth. The book and the telescope lay before him. He felt the future upon him. The vision of it was a choice to be made.

In its falling the rain seemed to rise up from the ground, and Gracian too had become as the rain, a slender line descending and yet rising, lifting upward yet drawn down to the earth, and finally then, as the rain soaked his hair, the tears came, the final release that his eyes could give, and the tears fell out of him like rain. He thought: *To be faithful to the chosen vision. To accept its failings. To unmoor the stars.* And with his hands he began to dig in